BORN OF AIR

AN ELEMENTAL ORIGINS NOVEL

D1570147

BORN OF AIR

AN ELEMENTAL ORIGINS NOVEL

A.L. KNORR

INTELLECTUALLY PROMISCUOUS PRESS

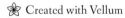 Created with Vellum

ALSO BY A.L. KNORR

Metal Angel

Mira's Return Series

Returning

Falling

Surfacing

The Kacy Chronicles

Descendant

Ascendant

Combatant

Transcendent

Join A.L. Knorr's VIP Reader List at www.alknorrbooks.com and she'll personally send you a reminder as soon as her next book is out.

If you want to find the secrets of the universe, think in terms of energy, frequency and vibration.

NIKOLA TESLA

PROLOGUE

Saltford, New Year's Eve 1998

THE NIGHT WAS cold and sharp, and the stars winked down from a black velvet sky, almost snapping with clarity. The main custodian of St. Joseph's Hospital for nearly twenty years had just reached into the pocket of his parka for the keys to his truck when the sound of footsteps pounding behind him made him turn.

"Amin, wait!" A red-faced nurse, out of breath and with a hand over her heart, reached him and put a hand on his shoulder.

"Steady on, Irene," said Amin, grasping her by the elbow, his bushy salt-and-pepper brows drawing together with concern. Irene was not a young woman anymore and her girth had increased over the twelve years she and Amin had worked together. She wouldn't be moving this fast without good reason. "Everything okay?"

Irene and Amin were two of only a handful of staff members at the hospital who called each other by their first names and paid no heed to the hierarchy that segregated most of the staff. It was the reason Irene had been sent to fetch Amin, and not some other nurse.

Irene shook her head, panting, her brow creased with worry. "I'm sorry, I know you're on your way home and it's New Year's Eve, but we have a situation we could use your help with."

"Of course." Amin waited while the nurse took a few more breaths to calm herself.

"We've got young woman in the ER who is in labor. She doesn't speak any English. We think her language might be Arabic, but it's difficult to tell. You speak Arabic, right?"

Amin frowned. "My parents did, but I've forgotten most of it."

"That's more than anyone else here can say. Would you please come and see if you can translate?"

Amin nodded and the two ran back to the hospital's rear entrance while Irene caught Amin up on some of the details. "A young couple heard sounds of distress coming from their back alley. They discovered her hiding in some brush there."

"Hiding?" Amin echoed, his brow furrowing.

"That's what they said," Irene huffed as they reached the door. Amin opened the doors and let her pass first. "They said it was all they could do to get her into their van. The only reason they got her here is because her water broke and she couldn't resist them any longer."

"Is she in her right mind?" Amin's heart had begun to pound, but not from the jog across the parking lot.

They donned paper booties and made their way down the hall toward the ER. Irene lowered her voice. "She's jumpier than a cat in a room full of rocking chairs. But her anxiety is only part of it. Her ankles and hands are swollen," Irene said. "We suspect she's pre-eclamptic."

Amin was a janitor, not a doctor, but he'd been working in the hospital for long enough to know exactly what that meant. His stomach dropped. If the young woman was pre-eclamptic this late in the game, there was very little that could be done to help her. The focus would be on saving the baby. Amin also knew that the young woman had not yet been properly admitted; if she had been, Irene wouldn't be allowed to tell him any of this.

"Is she homeless?"

Irene blew out a breath and shook her head, her cheeks ballooning. "You'll be able to answer that for all of us." They pushed their way into the ER and Amin came to a standstill.

The woman lying on the bed whipped her head toward them and gasped, cringing away from the door. Even with sweat beading her brow, she was a striking woman. She had a long neck and large dark eyes. Her swollen fingers were visible, wrapped over her belly. Expensive looking rings with large, colored stones graced her fingers, her puffy flesh pushing out on either side of the bands. It was likely the rings would have to be cut off. Diamond studs sparkled from her earlobes. Amin doubted the jewelry was fake. The woman reminded Amin of a sculpture he'd seen in a history textbook once called Nefertiti Bust. Her cheekbones were painfully high and her caramel skin was flawless save for wrinkles of pain and worry on her brow. Her dark hair was tied back in a bun at the nape of her neck, but damp flyaways had escaped and framed her face. Her lips were red and looked petal soft. She didn't appear to be a day over twenty. A soft black cloak of fine wool swaddled her pregnant form. Whatever shoes she'd had on had been removed. Amin could see the thickness of her swollen ankles above the elastic of the paper booties on her feet.

Medical staff rushed about, and equipment was clustered around the bed, including an ultrasound and a fetal monitor. Three more staff stood back against the wall, scrubbed and prepped and ready for a C-section if needed.

"Min 'anat?" she said in a dialect of Levantine Arabic. *Who are you?* Her voice quavered and concern swept over Amin like a heavy cloak.

Amin took a few steps forward, whipping the gray knit cap off his head. "My name is Amin," he said in halting Arabic, his face soft with compassion. "My Arabic is old," he apologized, "and a little different from yours."

"Did they send you?" Her arms closed protectively over her belly.

Amin was confused by this phrasing and thought perhaps he'd misunderstood her. His Arabic was pitifully rusty. "Nurse Irene came to get me because I speak a little Arabic," Amin replied, putting a hand out. "I'm a custodian here. What is your name?"

Her face softened, just a little, but she didn't answer. Amin watched her face tighten and transform into a mask of pain and she ducked her chin to her chest and groaned.

"Nurse," Amin said, feeling panic sneaking up on him. He'd never been good at seeing people in pain, especially women. "Help her."

"We're trying," answered one of the doctors. "That's why you're here. Can you convince her to let us get her out of her clothes? If we can at least get that far—"

Amin nodded. He relayed this to the woman. "Baby wants to come," he said gently in his rusty Arabic. "This is Irene," Amin put a hand on the nurse's shoulder. "She is a good nurse. She'd like to help you change."

To their relief, the woman nodded, still with her face down. She began to pant again.

"I'll be just outside," said Amin. On his way out the ER, Amin paused to tell the doctor, "She sounds Jordanian."

The doctor nodded. "Thanks, I'll make a note. That's helpful."

Amin ducked out of the room to allow them to undress the woman and get her into a proper hospital gown. He waited, twisting his hat into a wrinkled mess, until he was asked back in.

When he stepped into the room, the sound of a distant helicopter passing somewhere overhead made the woman cringe and her eyes dart to the window. She pinched her lips between her teeth as a keening sound rose in her throat. One of the ER nurses was drawing blood and put a hand on her shoulder to keep her still. All of the staff looked grave. Several IV lines had been inserted into the woman in

Amin's short absence, and snaked up from the bed to various bags of liquid.

"It's all right. It's just a—" Amin had to think before remembering there was no Arabic word for helicopter. He said the English word with an Arabic accent, *hilykubtr*. He approached the bed, as close as he thought she'd allow.

Amin asked the woman again. "Would you please tell us your name?"

She rolled her eyes up at him, panting. For a moment he thought she wouldn't answer. "Tala," she said, finally.

"Her name is Tala," said Amin to the staff. He smiled encouragingly at the young woman.

"Thank you," said one of the nurses.

"Tala," Irene echoed, rubbing Tala's back. "That's a girl. We're going to take good care of you."

Emboldened by the success of getting her first name. Amin tried for more information. "What is you family name? Is there someone we can contact for you? The father, perhaps?"

"No father!" the woman snapped as her face and body tightened again with another contraction. She opened her eyes to glare at him. "There was no father! Never a father! No more questions!"

Amin looked up at Irene, bemused. "She says there was never a father, and she doesn't want me to ask her any more questions."

"Never a father," echoed Irene. "That's a first."

"One of the symptoms of eclampsia is confusion," offered one of the other ER nurses.

"Either that or my Arabic is worse than I thought." Amin swallowed hard, looking at the young woman and feeling helpless.

"Best leave," said Irene. "We can't have her any more upset than she already is."

As Amin took his leave, the sounds of the woman's cries followed him down the hall. Amin paced in the waiting room just the way thousands of expectant fathers had done for forty years before him. Five and a half hours passed before Irene emerged. Midnight had passed and the new year had begun. Amin had barely noticed. He got up from his chair as Irene came through the double doors, and his back protested with a creak.

"I thought you'd gone home," Irene said. Her face was pale and drawn, her shoulders stooped with exhaustion.

"I was hoping I could help again, after the birth."

"Thank you, Amin. That's very kind." Irene rubbed a hand over her brow. "We lost her."

Amin sat back down, his body suddenly feeling too heavy for his legs.

"Nothing could be done. Team's trying to track down her records to see if she'd been admitted anywhere else, or possibly had a OBGYN in the city."

"And the baby?"

"Underweight, but otherwise okay. She'll be in intensive care for a little while."

"She. A little girl."

Irene nodded and retrieved a wrinkled piece of paper from her chest pocket. "Tala asked for a piece of paper and a pen shortly after you left."

"How?"

Irene made a gesture with her hands, which would have been perfect for a game of charades. Anyone of any language would have understood what it meant. Palm flat for paper and fingers grasping an invisible writing utensil.

"What does it mean?" Irene handed him the paper.

Amin unfolded the page to reveal the elegant swirls of Arabic, written by an unsteady hand. "Tala wrote this right after I left?"

Irene nodded. "Last thing she ever 'said.'"

"She must have seen a health professional at some point. She knew the baby was a girl. It's a name." He read the name aloud to the nurse.

ONE

"Petra Kara. What a treat," Noel said, standing up from behind his desk as I walked in. "I was so pleased when I saw you had booked an appointment." He straightened his suit jacket and bounced a little on his toes.

I smiled at my old therapist. "Nice to see you too, Mr. Pierce."

His office hadn't changed. Old wooden paneling covered in dusty paintings of ships and sunsets lined the walls, wherever there weren't bookshelves bursting with psychology titles. Tall warped windows with small, diamond-shaped panes blurred and rattled slightly at the rain beating down on them outside. The forest-green carpet was worn by years of feet scuffing across it, creating a lighter green path from the door, circling the space between the couches and chairs, around his desk, and out the door again. The smell of Old Spice cologne made me remember the young, scared kid I'd been when I first met Noel Pierce. He had been my assigned therapist throughout my years in foster care, and while I had resisted him at first, like most kids did, he had been patient with me. He'd come to earn my trust, and if I was really honest, I'd missed him since I'd become of legal age and left the system.

He waved a hand and circled his desk, gesturing for me to sit in one of the plush chairs. "Please, don't go back to all that. We've been through too much for you to call me Mr. Pierce."

He waited for me to sit, and then sat down facing me. He crossed one leg over the other and folded his hands in his lap.

"Sure. Noel," I said, settling into a chair I was very familiar with. This meeting did feel a little bit different from when I'd been a minor. Instead of being a government-funded patient and ward of the childcare system, I was coming to Noel as a legal adult and paying for this session with my own money. I sure hoped it was worth it.

The paper in my jeans pocket crinkled as I sat down. On it were the three bullet points I'd come to discuss today.

"You've been out of foster care for over a year now," Noel said. "You aren't obliged to come and see me any more." He peered over his wire-rimmed glasses at me.

"I know," I swallowed and cleared my throat. "But I need some help with something and you were the only person I could think to talk to." He was also the only person who was sworn to patient confidentiality. Noel was *forbidden* to spill the secrets I was about to share with him.

"Well." He spread his hands out, looking pleased. "I'm flattered. What's going on?"

I knotted my fingers and put them on my lap, not quite sure how to begin.

Sensing my hesitation, Noel offered, "Why don't you catch me up on the last eighteen months. I understand you're working at the Maritime History Museum?"

I nodded. "I started working there just after Christmas 2015 while finishing up high school. I still work there, but I've finally graduated from just ticket sales to ticket sales and tour groups."

"Well," Noel nodded his approval. "This is wonderful. Well done, Petra."

"Thanks," I said, but I had to shove down the annoyance that threatened to rise whenever people patronized me. I didn't bother mentioning that I had also started a dog-walking service. Exercising pets and working at the local museum was a far cry from where I wanted to be. "I had applied to Cambridge University—"

"I remember," Noel murmured.

I nodded. Of course he did. He was the one who had to listen to me cry on the phone after I'd been accepted into their Archaeology Undergrad program but couldn't go because there was no way I could afford it. Even with the scholarship I'd won and the savings that Beverly, my foster mom, had set aside for me before her death, I had still been dismally short of funds.

"I took the year off to work and save, and I'll be applying again in October," I explained. "For January 2018."

Noel frowned and rested his chin on a hand. "We have perfectly good schools here in Canada."

"I know. But—"

"You want the best," he finished.

"I've been dreaming of Cambridge since I was a little girl. Stephen Hawking, David Attenborough, Alan Turing." I named off the famous alumni on my fingers. "Prince Zeid Bin Ra'ad, the Jordanian Prince and UN High Commissioner for Human Rights went there." I raised my eyebrows for emphasis.

Noel was nodding. He already knew that my birth mother had been Jordanian. His expression said he didn't find the link very compelling.

"Not the least of which are Gertrude Caton-Thompson, Dorothy Garrod, and Winifred Lamb," I went on, my voice growing energized at the thought of following in the footsteps of these pioneering women of archaeology—my heroes and role models.

"Don't forget at least six known Soviet spies," Noel murmured over his fingers.

"Very funny."

"But why, Petra?" Noel straightened. "Why is it so important to study at Cambridge? You could already be studying at any number of very good Canadian Universities as we speak. Your grades are top notch, at least from grade nine onwards. I'm certain if you applied for funding—"

"It has to be Cambridge. If there is one thing Beverly left me with," I said, my voice breaking over the name of my deceased foster mother and the only real parent I had ever known, "it's that I had to do whatever I chose to do to the best of my ability."

"I don't think she meant you had to go to the best school—" Noel injected.

"But I *have* the grades," I said, shifting forward in my seat. "I *did* get in. Money is the only problem, almost. I'm so close I can taste it!"

"All right, all right." Noel made patting motions on the air the way he did whenever I was getting too riled up. "Yes, okay. I understand. And congratulations on being accepted."

"Thank you," I said.

"So then, now what? What's your plan?"

"I have worked all during my gap year at the museum. I've been saving up and studying on my own—" And living in a drafty, tiny apartment on the seedy side of town, I added in my head. Where the pipes rattled in the winter like Jacob Marley with his chains, the windows leaked, and the smell of weed was ever present from my neighbors.

"How much do you need?"

"About 20,000," I said.

"Oh," Noel sounded pleasantly surprised. I knew what he was thinking, and I didn't have to probe his mind to do it. Beverly had left me close to ten grand. If I'd been working and saving for a year, then it wasn't an unachievable sum.

"Pounds," I added.

"Oh." This time the tone was disappointed.

"Per year," I finished, with a slight wince.

He closed his eyes. "Petra," he began. "By the time you count your undergrad, and your master's, a PhD could be a ten-year commitment."

"I've already got a year and half's worth saved up," I interjected, speaking quickly.

"Almost?" he said, his face going still.

"What?"

"You said money is the only problem, *almost*," he reminded me. Noel might be slow to pick up on things, but it was guaranteed that he *would* pick them up.

"Well, there's also the matter of wanting to go on an Old World dig," I added, a little weakly. I began to play with the frayed threads at the rip in my Salvation Army jeans.

"An *Old World* dig?"

"Cambridge doesn't require dig experience, but I'm most interested in historical archaeology—archaeology with the aid of written documents. An Old World excavation on my resume would give me a huge boost." Opportunities for international digs were out there, but most of them required payment for a place on the dig. I couldn't afford that. Ideally, I would be able to find a dig on which I could volunteer.

"What's the problem?" Noel raised his eyebrows. "You've been a volunteer on excavations before."

"I have, but they were through Mr. Hatley, at the museum."

Noel laughed. "You make it sound like you were bored to tears. What's wrong with Mr. Hatley? He's a perfectly sound connection."

"Mr. Hatley arranges New World pre-historic digs. He's not like... David," I said, slowly, dropping my chin and leveling him with a meaningful look.

I watched the understanding cross his face like dawn sunlight sweeping across a landscape. "I can't do that, Petra," he said, his expression regretful.

"But I don't know anyone else who knows anyone," I said, putting my hands together in prayer. "Just a phone call, that's all I'm asking."

Noel sighed and his eyes closed briefly. I could almost hear him counting to five. Noel's brother David was an archaeologist and he was on a huge excavation right now, one I would give almost anything to be a part of. It wasn't the first time I had asked.

Sensing his hesitation, I pushed harder. "I can accept it if he says no. All I'm asking for is an opportunity to talk with him." I took a breath and added, "Or meet him."

Noel shook his head. "I'm truly sorry, Petra, you know I would do anything for you that was within my power."

"This *is* within your power." I tried to keep the pleading tone from my voice and failed. Miserably.

Noel folded his hands with obvious patience. "Petra, do you know where David is working right now?"

"East of Baghdad," I said without so much as a breath between his question and my answer.

Noel froze and blinked as though surprised that I knew. "Yes," he said, "and do I have to remind you where that is?" He peered at me from over the tops of his wire-rimmed spectacles.

"Iraq," I said, nonplussed. "He's helping to salvage a site damaged by the Gulf War."

Noel's voice went breathy, as though the meaning should be clear. "Yes."

I let out a long breath, too. I did know exactly what he was saying. Iraq was one of the most war-torn and unstable countries to travel in right now. There was no way any team leader worth his salt would take a prospective student in the last year of her teens with him on an excavation, even if it was sanctioned by Iraqi antiquities. The thing was, I really didn't care about the danger. I cared about the *history*.

"Why don't you talk to Mr. Hatley at the museum again," Noel suggested. "He'll have some other Canadian connections you can tap in to." His voice sounded overly delighted at this idea.

I frowned. "I'm not interested in digging up arrowheads and lithics."

"Lithics?"

"The stone tools used by Paleo-Indians." I leaned forward

earnestly. "I want a real excavation. Something *ancient*. Something Phoenician, or Egyptian, or Neo-Punic."

I looked at the clock on Noel's desk. Half my time was gone and I hadn't even gotten to the important stuff yet. One topic down, two to go. If he couldn't help me by connecting me to his brother, maybe he could help me with my other problems. I cleared my throat. "There's another issue that I wanted to talk to you about today. Two actually, but they're linked. I think."

Relieved, Noel retrieved a kerchief from his pocket and mopped his brow. "By all means. What's bothering you?"

My heart sped up but there was no backing down now. I was about to spill a secret I hadn't shared with anyone in my entire life, not even Beverly, and I had no idea how Noel was going to take it. My fingertips grew cool, even as my body temperature seemed to rise. I pulled at the collar of my t-shirt and took a breath.

"I can read minds."

"Sorry." Noel laughed. "I thought you said you could read minds." He coughed uncomfortably into a closed fist. "I must've misunderstood you. Could you repeat that please?"

"You didn't misunderstand."

The air grew thick between us as we sat there looking at one another, me fighting the urge to dig at his thoughts. How was he reacting inside? Noel's face had become impassive. It was the kind of expression I'd seen on him before. He trusted me and knew that I wasn't a liar, yet he wasn't sure he could believe me. My heart sank. It wasn't the reaction I'd been hoping for.

"You've never encountered a mind-reader before?"

"Petra," he said, his face very still. "Telepathy is a pseudoscience. It has never been demonstrated to exist."

I frowned. "I know that. I have done my research. I was just hoping that maybe you had access to information that I don't. So, you don't know how I can get rid of it?" Great. I had spilled my secret for nothing. "Do you have any experience with telekinesis?" I added, taking another chance.

He blinked rapidly, like he'd gotten dust in his eyes. "Telekinesis is also a pseudoscience." He rubbed the bridge of his nose where his specs sat, like they were pinching him. It was a tell. He didn't believe me. My heart felt heavy. The one adult left in my life that I thought I could go to with anything was probably now questioning my sanity.

"Have you been under a lot of pressure lately?" he asked, hooking his interlaced fingers over a knee.

"No more than usual." I sighed. I went to get up from the chair. "I guess we're done." As far as I was concerned, if Noel couldn't offer me any additional information about my condition, then I wasn't going to find what I needed here.

Noel got to his feet as well, and rather quickly for a portly chap. "Petra, please sit down. You can't drop a bomb on me like that and not explain. I promise, I will try to help you."

I sank back into my seat, hesitantly. I rubbed my hands together to warm them. Disappointment wormed its way into my gut. I tried not to let it show on my face. Noel was the only card I had to play; there was no one else that I could go to for help.

"I knew it could be a mistake telling you," I said. "But I thought that you of all people might have some idea how to stop it. After all, you see all kinds come through here. People with all sorts of mental health problems."

He gave a chuckle. "Not like this. Why do you want to stop it?" Now he was mining for gold. Keep the patient talking. Psychology 101.

I was game. It was what I'd come here for.

"Because it's annoying," I said. "The movies make telepathy out to be some sort of great power, something that's supposed to give you a one-up in this world. The reality of it is much different, let me tell you."

Noel scooted forward on the couch and propped an elbow on the arm of his chair. "What is the reality of it?"

I made a face and crossed my arms over my chest. "Do you have any idea how unintelligent most of humanity is? How selfish, simple, and vapid? I have no interest in sharing my mental real estate with someone else's idiotic thoughts."

It had been agonizing as a child, before I had a strategy in place to protect my mind from other people's self-talk and mental images. The wall I had put up was better than it had ever been, but sometimes random thoughts not of my making would leak through, usurping my own thinking.

"Other people's thoughts are almost never enlightening. They always take me backward. Do you have any idea how quickly I'll devolve if I go around picking up other people's mental garbage? It's like..." I paused, searching for the words to explain how it felt. "Pollution. Noise cluttering up a library that's supposed to be serene and peaceful. When I was a kid, I thought I was crazy. I was seven years old when I finally figured out what was wrong with me."

Noel's face was alight with an expression of fascination, and I could almost believe that he believed me. "What happened? What happened to make you understand?"

"I was able to match up a random image that had popped into my head with the thoughts of the caseworker who was interviewing me," I explained. "We were supposed to be going over my report cards and talking about how well I was integrating into a new school. She'd ask me questions and I'd answer them. But whenever I began to talk, the image of a man wearing a navy uniform and black horn-rimmed glasses would materialize in my mind and completely derail me. I didn't know who he was. I had never seen him before. It was frightening."

I didn't say it out loud to Noel, but it had gotten even worse when the man began to kiss me passionately and then swept me off my feet. Somewhere in the midst of the shock of all that weirdness, I could sense an underlying urgency and pleasure that didn't belong to me. I had been too young to understand it.

"It wasn't until after the session was over," I continued, "and I watched the caseworker greet her husband in the parking lot, that I understood what I had been seeing." I shifted in my seat, folding my hands in my lap so I didn't fidget. The memory still made me uncomfortable. "He had just gotten back from overseas and she had missed him terribly. She couldn't wait to see him, and her mind kept drifting to him during our conversation."

"That's very sweet." Noel's expression was soppy.

"Not when you don't know what the hell is going on," I snapped.

He put his hands out. "Fair enough. Do the thoughts always come through in images?"

"Not always. Sometimes they come through as words. I guess it depends how the person is thinking in that moment."

"Could I ask you to show me?"

I knew that this would have to be part of it. "Okay," I said, already resigned. "Give me a moment."

Lifting the wall I had placed around my thoughts was a strange feeling, unpleasant. It was like my eyes had been focused on something very close to my face for hours and when I finally lifted them to the horizon, everything was horribly fuzzy. It might take a second or two for eyes to adjust and there might be a little vertigo to go along with it. But it took my brain longer than that to home in on his thoughts. I closed my eyes as my vision blurred. The old, familiar pain throbbed low at the base of my neck. "Are you ready for this?" I asked, opening my eyes.

Noel looked relaxed, interested, unconcerned. "Okay." He leaned back against his chair. "What am I thinking about?"

I received his stream of consciousness and images began to form into my head, creeping in at the edges at first. Then they expanded like balloons in the middle of my skull, fully formed and in technicolor. Apparently, Noel was thinking visually.

"I see a rose garden." I closed my eyes. I couldn't help but smile at the beautiful image. "Looks like tea roses, mostly in pastels. They're at their peak and they must smell amazing. At the edge of the garden is an old stone railing with curved spindles and carved faces sitting on top. About a dozen of them, all with their backs to a very blue ocean."

I opened my eyes. "Some of the faces are cracked and worn, missing their noses."

Noel's complexion had gone pale, dewy with sweat. He had to believe me now. He was clearly shaken.

"It's a beautiful place," I added, still smiling. "Where is it?" I tried not to feel smug at his reaction. At least now there was no doubt that I was telling the truth.

He tried to reply but it came out as a dry wisp of a word. He coughed to clear his throat and tried again. "Ravello, Italy," he said. "The Terrace of Infinity. It was once owned by Beckett, the poet."

"Lovely," I murmured. I was about to congratulate him on how steady his imagination held the place he was thinking of. Most people's minds skittered from seemingly random images, to random worries, out of control like a runaway elephant. But just as I opened my mouth, the image of the side of a black handgun came flying at my face and seemed to bounce off my forehead. The weapon was gripped by a meaty, masculine hand. As the gun made contact, there was a flash of red. While I didn't feel any physical pain, I jerked backward, startled, as I picked up the violent memory from Noel.

"What was that?" I gripped the armrests of my chair, alarmed. Fear riddled the image with wavy lines, like heat coming off blacktop on a summer day. I had never seen terror warp a thought so badly.

So, even Noel had trouble controlling his thoughts, as that was definitely something he wouldn't have wanted me to see. Thoughts were strange. If you try not to think of a giraffe, the first thing that will pop into your head is a giraffe. Obviously, Noel now believed me and the fear of me seeing one of his worst memories came rushing to the forefront of his mind. I'd picked it up precisely because he'd been afraid that I would.

"Stop, stop!" He put a hand out. His eyes were wide.

I slammed down the gate between my mind and his. The feeling of it was so violent, it jarred my molars. The foggy images filtering into my mind ceased. The dull pain at the base of my skull eased and disappeared, but my heart was pounding.

That last thought I had picked up was the most shocking, disconcerting one I had ever picked up from anyone. Why was my mildmannered therapist being beaten by a man with a gun? Fury flared hot and hard inside me and I had to take a deep breath. Noel wouldn't hurt a fly. This was another reason I didn't like to know other people's thoughts, especially if it was someone I cared about. If they were in some kind of trouble, I couldn't help but get involved. For all I knew, that thought was thirty years old and had long since been resolved. "Are you in some kind of trouble?"

He shook his head as he pulled at his tie, loosening it from around his neck. "Don't worry about me," he wheezed. As though he were the one who could read minds, he added, "It's a very old memory. Resolved a long time ago." He was a little out of breath and wouldn't meet my eyes. "I apologize," he said. "I'm sorry I didn't believe you." He said this while shucking his suit jacket. Sweat circles darkened the fabric of his purple shirt. "Would you like a drink? I need a drink."

"Yes, please." Now that my mind was sealed, my heart was slowing down.

Noel went to the sideboard under the window and poured two glasses of water from the pitcher sitting there. I watched his hand shake and the water slosh. He returned to our little circle of furniture and handed me a glass.

"Thanks." I took it and drank. I set the glass on a coaster on the coffee table between us.

"Can you still read my mind?" Noel crossed over to his chair, looking down at me. He tapped his fingers against his glass, nervously.

I frowned. His voice had a tremor I didn't like. He was afraid of me. "No, you asked me to stop and I did." Reading minds was an invasion of privacy at the deepest level. Doing it made me feel sick, not physically, aside from the dull headache, but emotionally sick. I felt like a criminal, a voyeur, someone with a serious mental health problem.

He settled back in his chair, his shirt damp and his necktie gaping. The top two buttons of his shirt were undone. His eyes met mine for the first time, narrowing as he stared at me. His gaze was laced with suspicion.

"I'm not." I held his gaze. Then I realized that my defensive words made it sound like I was. "I can tell by your face that you don't believe me. But I'm not. I swear on Beverly's memory." I put a hand over my heart.

His mouth twitched. "You don't have to do that. I believe you." His face relaxed and he took a kerchief from his chest pocket and mopped his brow. "How are you able to control it?"

"Years of practice." I relaxed as Noel relaxed, sitting back in my chair and letting my shoulders fall. "Mostly it involves not thinking about the fact that I can do it and genuinely not wanting to know what people are thinking. If I find myself *wanting* to know someone's thoughts, that's when it takes real effort. It's like holding up a stone dam with your bare hands. It's tiring, and if you have to do it for a long time eventually some water will leak through. If that makes any sense."

Noel nodded, still pale. "It does. Why didn't you tell me earlier? Why now?"

"I don't like being looked at like I'm nuts. Not that you would." I put up a hand. "But most people would. And I'm not interested in having to prove myself. I just find I still have leakage sometimes. As I prepare to go into university, I'd like to get rid of it. You can imagine the battle of will that ensues during an exam," I explained. "It's the reason I always studied so hard. I didn't want to put myself in a position where I'd be tempted to cheat." I shrugged. "I was hoping you might have some experience with it from other patients. But I guess not."

"Sorry to disappoint you, Petra," Noel said. "This is a first for me." He took a breath. "And the telekinesis you mentioned?"

"Yes. What about it?"

Noel looked uncomfortable. "You have... you are..." He adjusted his glasses. "You have this ability, too?"

I nodded. "It's not as much of an issue, but I brought it up because I thought the two might be linked."

"Can you...?" He invited me to demonstrate with a gesture.

I nodded and picked up my glass, drained it of water and set it back on the table. On the wood this time, not the coaster. I sat back in my chair and folded my arms over my stomach. Without taking my eyes from Noel, I gave the glass a gentle mental shove at its base so it didn't tip over.

My glass slid across the table and clinked into his.

Noel's hand flew to cover his mouth.

"Cheers," I said, trying to lighten the atmosphere.

Noel's gaze flew to my face. I watched him make an effort to get his shock under control, but his complexion was waxy and he was still sweating. The sound of his palm scraping against his stubble was loud and filled the room.

I sighed and glanced at the clock on his desk. "We're out of time." I got to my feet. "I hope I haven't ruffled you too much. I know you have another patient right after me."

"No, no." Noel made a 'calm-down' gesture. "I—I'm fine."

But he wasn't. It was plain on his face. No one needed telepathy to see how much I'd shaken him.

"I'm sorry, Noel," I said quietly. "If I had known..." I bounced a fist off my thigh, feeling awkward. "I wouldn't have..." I sighed. What else could I say?

"It's fine, it's fine." Noel got to his feet as well. "I've just never seen anything like it. Would you like to make another appointment?" He followed me as I walked to the door. I plucked my rain jacket off the coatrack and picked up my purse. "There would be no charge. I'd really like to help you with this."

But he couldn't. He'd already shown me that. I gave him a smile but it felt stiff and unnatural on my face. "I don't think so. Thanks anyway." I reached for the door handle.

"Wait, Petra—" But he seemed to be out of words for now. Couldn't blame him.

I opened the door. "Nice to see you again, Noel. I wish you well." I stepped out onto the landing and closed the door quietly behind me. As I stepped out of Noel's office building and into the driving rain, I wondered if I was doomed to alienate anyone I ever let in. Sharing my true self seemed like an impossibility.

TWO

Passing through the museum foyer for my shift early the following morning, I stopped to scan the community bulletin board like I did every week. Rarely was there anything more interesting than an afternoon seminar on navigating by the constellations, or someone hawking their grandmother's pearl jewelry. But when my eyes fell on a new posting, one that I was certain hadn't been there the day before, I felt my world shift on its axis.

Are you passionate about ancient history? Looking for excavation experience to add to your resume? University students of archaeology are welcome to apply for a volunteer position on our summer dig team. Must be available for a consecutive six-week period. Airfare and accommodation will be provided. 3 positions available.

I snatched the posting from the bulletin board like it was seconds from going up in smoke. My eyes devoured the words three times and the name and phone number at the bottom was now emblazoned on my memory for all time. Field Director—Ethan Rich.

I often joked that I knew everyone in Saltford who had any connection to the museum or so much as a passing interest in archaeology, but I had never heard of Ethan Rich. Who was he? The phone number was local, but the logo and the association were completely foreign to me. Society for the Preservation of Archaeological Treasures, sponsored by The Group of Winterthür.

I left the foyer and made a beeline for the ticket desk where Danielle sat chewing gum and filing her nails. Danielle was a twenty-something university dropout who had won the job in ticketing through, well, I called it nepotism, she called it her "family network." Danielle's aunt had been the museum's curator for over a decade.

"When did this go up?" I held up the bulletin.

Danielle drew her eyes from her thumbnail with what seemed like monumental effort. She gave a loud snap of her gum and lifted a shoulder. "Don't know. People stick stuff up there all the time. It's free."

"Yes, I know it's free. But do you know who put it up? Did you talk to them?"

She wrinkled her brow. "There was a guy. Day before yesterday I think."

This is why I didn't like to read minds. Even if I had been interested in probing Danielle's mind for a face or an interaction linked to the posting, she'd remember it all wrong and it would just throw me off. The human mind was a fallible thing. I didn't trust the capabilities of human memory, not even my own.

I passed Danielle and went into the office behind the ticket counter. I closed the door, hung up my jacket, and sat at the desk. I pulled the phone toward me, selected a line, and raised my finger to punch in the number on the advertisement.

The door cracked open and Danielle's pale freckled face poked in. "Mr. Hatley doesn't like you making personal calls on the museum phone."

"He won't mind this one," I replied, shouldering the receiver. "It's work-related."

Her statement was untrue anyway. Mr. Hatley knew I didn't have a cell phone and had personally invited me to use the phone in his office anytime I needed it. Mr. Hatley was nearly as invested in manifesting my future career as an archaeologist as I was. Once he'd seen how careful I was with money and my single-minded desire to get to Cambridge, he'd thrown all his oars behind me.

I shot Danielle a look and she rolled her eyes and shut the door, leaving me alone.

I dialed the number on the ad and the line rang in my ear, once, twice.

"Yes?" A man's voice.

"I'm looking for Mr. Ethan Rich, please."

"At your service."

My heart did a somersault and my fingers gripped the receiver. "I'm calling about your post requesting volunteers for a dig this summer."

"Ah. We've one position left to fill. Are you a student of archaeology?"

"I'm hoping to attend Cambridge University's Archaeology program next January."

"Cambridge. Well!" He sounded suitably impressed. "But you haven't begun yet?"

"No. I took a year off to save money."

"How old are you?"

"Nineteen." I had just turned only three months before.

"Mmmm. You're a little on the young and inexperienced side. Perhaps if you wait a year or two. We will have openings for volunteers every year."

"But I need it," I began, and then stopped myself. The secret to helping myself get what I wanted was to give *him* what *he* wanted. And what he was looking for was a competent and valuable team member. "Where will you be digging?"

"Libya."

My heart did a backflip, as this caught me by surprise. North Africa. Marvelous. My mind raced through my knowledge of Libyan geography and history. I took a stab in the dark. "Sabratha?"

He chuckled. "Nowhere quite that glamorous. We'll be in the Acacus."

"The mountains in the south?" This was even better than Sabratha. Most of the Acacus was remote and undiscovered. Excitement flared in my gut.

"That's right."

"Your bulletin didn't specify, but might you by chance be studying in the area of the black mummy?"

He paused. "How do you know about that?"

I let out a pent-up breath and smiled. "There is a relatively new theory that it was not the Egyptians that first used mummification. Seems to be the topic of most of the white papers coming out on Libya these days."

"That's true," he said. "We're not studying mummification, but our excavation isn't very far from where the black mummy was found." He paused. "What did you say your name was?"

"I didn't," I replied with a grin. Now we were getting somewhere. "But it's Petra Kara."

"Your name is Petra?"

"Yes. And yes, I was named after the ancient city." This was one of the few things I did know to be true from my childhood. My biological mother had given me the name after the beautiful desert city built by the Nabataeans. "My mother was from Jordan."

"But she settled in Saltford?"

"She passed away when I was born."

"Oh, I'm sorry."

"It's all right." If I had a dime for every time someone apologized for my mother's death, I could have paid Cambridge's tuition twice over. I hadn't even known her.

"Well, Miss Kara. We have never taken a teenage volunteer before, but you are legally an adult and you sound interested and interesting. Can you bring your resume by my office sometime in the next two days? We can have a little chat. I'm free between three and six either day."

With thinly disguised glee, I said I would and scribbled down the address he gave me. I hung up the phone and tapped my fingers on the table, giddy. It was perfect. It was as though fate had handed this opportunity to me on a platter. Libya. It was better than I could have even hoped for. It was ancient. It was expenses paid and it was this spring. I got up and left the office in search of Mr. Hatley, the posting in my hand. I'd need to give him a heads up that I'd likely need some time off.

ON MY WAY home from the museum, I was so distracted by the possibility of going on an actual archaeological dig that I made a mistake that I hadn't made in over a year. Instead of pedaling my rusty town bicycle (which used to be yellow but was now mostly bare steel and rust) through the park and down the back alley of my building, I went to Victoria Street. I was halfway down the block when I realized my mistake and applied the brakes. There, its two front windows with the shades at half-mast, looking like a half-asleep Lego-giant, was my old house. Beverly's old house.

Beverly Hames had been my last foster parent, my best foster parent, and the only mother I ever really knew. A spinster with a gruff manner but a big heart had taken me in as a temporary foster child and I'd ended up staying with her until she died. Beverly was strict with me for the first little while. No scratching my itches in public, no leaving my bed unmade, no cursing.

Beverly had chosen to renovate my bedroom to expand the closet and replace soggy floor-boards. During that time, we had shared her room. At first, I thought she intended to put me on the squeaky pull-out sofa in her living room. I didn't want to sleep in the living room. I hated the otherworldly glow the streetlights cast in the front windows. The traffic going slowly by the house never failed to rouse me from even the deepest sleep. It wasn't the sound of the cars engines that woke me, but the random thoughts of the drivers that drifted into my dreams like fog. I had been only ten at the time but by then I knew what those random images and vignettes were.

As though it was Beverly who could read minds, she set up a cot in her bedroom with flannel sheets and one of her handmade quilts. I breathed a sigh of relief. I was used to being around Beverly's mind. It rarely snuck up on me and if it did, her thoughts were never disturbing. More often than not, they had something to do with looking after me.

I gripped my bike's handlebars, remembering how I had woken in the pitch black of her bedroom, her blackout curtains blocking out all light. I'd needed to pee but didn't want to wake Beverly, so I'd ignored the lamp she'd placed on the floor beside my cot. I toed my way slowly in the direction of the door, hands out, blindly feeling in front of me for the doorknob. I'd bumped an elbow against the open closet door, and then tripped over the fan in the corner.

"Just turn on the light, pet," Beverly had mumbled from her cocoon of blankets, her voice heavy and sweet with sleep. "It's quieter."

I had smiled in the dark. Turning on the light would wake her for certain, but she'd rather I wake her up than smash my toes against something unforgiving. She had a way of saying *I love you* without ever saying the words. Her 'I love you's' were found home-cooked, steaming, and fragrant on my plate every day, or in the fridge and ready to be heated if she wasn't going to be home for some reason. Her 'I love you's' were the previously holey socks that would appear darned and tucked into my laundry basket, lined up like sleeping mice. Her 'I love you' was the homely face in the back of the crowd at my school recitals, her warm brown eyes approving and her expression proud.

Life with Beverly had been simple and safe. Both of us being introverted and studious meant not much talk filled the air. Winter evenings found me curled up with a history text and Beverly either reading her Bible or knitting something useful—mittens, a scarf, or a brightly colored tea-cozy. The soft clacking of her knitting needles became my white noise and for a time, after her death, I found it difficult to read without it.

Beverly was admitted to the hospital just after Halloween when a blinding headache took her sight away. She'd had headaches a lot that year, but being Beverly Hames meant she didn't go to the hospital unless she'd chopped off a finger. She would take some medication and go to bed, and most times the pounder would slink back to wherever it came from. Turned out that where it had come from was an 8.25-centimeter inoperable tumor. She never recovered her sight and she never left the hospital. She passed away twelve days after my seventeenth birthday. It still hurt. Maybe it would never stop hurting.

At seventeen, I was not yet considered a legal adult, but my caseworker convinced the board that I was responsible enough to live on my own, with support from them, until I turned eighteen. They paid for a comfortable basement suite near the high school and gave me an allowance for living expenses. When I turned eighteen, all of that stopped. That was when I moved into my drafty old studio in the apartment complex.

The wind put its cold lips against my neck and I shivered, pulling my collar up around my ears as I stared at my old house. One of the curtains moved and a child's dirty face poked out. I smiled at her and she stared back with no expression. The child's mother appeared shortly with a washcloth in hand, to tackle the girl's face.

I bore down on the pedals and redirected for home. Beverly Hames didn't live there any more, and neither did I.

THREE

The address Ethan had given me led me to a small bungalow in an older neighborhood of Saltford. A cold, sloppy rain had blown in off the Atlantic so I drove my beat-up 1991 Toyota Tercel stick-shift to the meeting.

"Come on, baby." I patted the steering wheel while turning the key. The car coughed to life and I grinned. "When I said I'd drive you into the ground, I meant it. Better than rusting in a scrap yard. Don't you think?"

I had used some of the money Beverly left me to buy the old car after I'd graduated high school. I used my bike all summer unless I had to go somewhere across the city, but during the freezing Atlantic winters, a car was an absolute necessity. I had also paid for a block-heater to be installed, and it was the best money I had ever spent after one year of driving for part of the winter without one. I still had to wear gloves to handle the steering wheel but at least my feet no longer turned into ice-cubes and my breath didn't hang in the air in front of my face. My hope these days was that nothing on the car would break until I made the move to England for school.

I killed the car outside of a navy bungalow with a red door and got out. Pulling my hat down over my ears, I scampered up the walkway and onto the front porch to ring the doorbell. The March afternoon was bitingly cold and the damp put shivers right into my bones.

A shape appeared through the frosted glass in the door and it swung open to reveal a portly man with a trim white beard and thick glasses with red rims. He wore plain khaki pants and a wool turtle-neck the color of emeralds.

"You must be Miss Kara." He swung the door open and stepped to the side. "I'm Ethan Rich. Come in, come in. It's wretchedly cold and wet today, isn't it?"

"Thanks, yes indeed." I stepped inside and took off my frosty hat and damp gloves. I extended a hand and we shook.

"Let me take your things and hang them by the fire," he said as I wormed out of my jacket. I handed him my coat and hat and followed him into a sitting room where a large window overlooked the front yard. A fire crackled in the narrow fireplace where overstuffed chairs had been pulled close. Ethan draped my things over a quilt rack and gestured to one of the chairs. "Have a seat."

"Thanks." I opened my backpack and pulled out my resume, care-fully preserved inside a plastic sheet protector. I handed it to him. "My resume and letters of recommendation. I've worked at the nautical museum here in Saltford for almost two years now. Do you know Mr. Hatley?" I sat in one of the chairs and crossed my ankles.

Ethan took my resume and peered at it through his bifocals. "I haven't had the pleasure, I'm afraid. I'm not from here. Our sponsor has set me up here in Saltford to organize the dig, but I'm actually from Toronto." He slid my resume and letters out of the sheet and I waited patiently while he scanned them. "Well, Miss Kara—"

"Call me Petra, please."

"Sure, and you can call me Ethan." He looked at me over the tops of his glasses. "Quite an impressive presentation you have here for one so young."

"Thank you."

He slid my papers back into the protector. "May I keep these?"

"Of course."

He set them on the small coffee table between us and sat back in his chair. "When did you become interested in archaeology as a profession?"

"It's the only thing I have ever wanted to do. For as long as I can remember, I've been fascinated by history. Every era is interesting to me, but I am drawn to the beginning of recorded history up to the Postclassical era. As you can imagine, your upcoming excavation in Libya got me very excited." I scooted forward to the edge of the couch. "What else do you need to know about me to grant me your final spot?"

Ethan chuckled. "It's yours. I have a feeling that you'll be an excellent addition to the team."

A grin split my face. "Really?"

"I'll lay out the situation for you and if you still want to come, we'll consider the position filled."

I couldn't imagine any situation that would make me not want to go on this dig, but I nodded and sat back in the chair. It was all I could do not to grin at Ethan stupidly as he walked me through the details.

"As I mentioned on the phone, this excavation takes place in the Acacus mountain range, not far from the city of Ghat. The volunteer positions are obviously not paid but all of the expenses are covered, including flights. Do you anticipate any issues getting six weeks off work this spring?"

"I already discussed the possibility with Mr. Hatley, and my dog-walking service is easily suspended. It won't be a problem." The only problem was that I wouldn't be making any money while I was away and this would put me behind in my savings schedule. I'd have to pick up a third job when I returned to make up for it.

Ethan went on. "It's a privately funded dig, done in association with my own little non-profit as well as the partnership of an antiquities authority in Libya. Excavations in Libya have been at a minimum these past several years, simply because of the civil unrest. But we've been granted permission from Libyan authorities, along with a security team. Every precaution has been taken to minimize risks." He snugged his glasses up his nose and raised bushy white brows. "Do you have any concerns about traveling to Libya?"

I shook my head. I would have gone to any number of dangerous places for excavation experience of this type.

Ethan laughed at my enthusiasm. "You remind me a bit of myself when I was your age. I would have gone into a black hole for the right dig."

"Sounds about right." I smiled. "What can you tell me about the site?"

"You'll learn all about that at our next team meeting, but I can give you some highlights. A skull was discovered near a cave system in the Acacus, initially by a paleontologist. The find was then reported to the police in Ghat. It takes some time to determine how old the remains are, but it was eventually confirmed to be ancient. As you know, archaeology is a very destructive process. We needed a very good reason to convince the Libyans and our sponsors that this dig is worthwhile. The skull proved interesting enough." He spread his hands. "So here we are. The area is marked by beautiful basalt monoliths and the rock-art that the Tadrart Acacus is known for. Test pits were dug in the sand where the skull was found. An old water source was discovered along with what we believe are the remains of walls and foundations...and what we're hoping are several grave sites."

My heart pounded so hard I could feel it in my temples. The excavation of human remains was what I most dreamed of. There was so much to be learned if this site really did turn out to be a grave. Ethan was still talking and I shook myself and focused, threading my hands in my lap to keep my fingers from trembling.

"There is a team at the site already, using GPR to flag anomalies and to stake out the excavation. By the time we arrive, we should be able to walk on site and excavate properly."

"A tag team effort?"

"That's right."

"Where is the funding coming from? I noted the name of the sponsor. The Group of Winterthür, who are they?"

Ethan nodded. "We're very lucky that someone on their board has taken a personal interest in the dig site. Winterthür is in Switzerland, but the group is made up of people from all nations. It's basically a global think tank that deals with international issues." He leaned in conspiratorially, as though sharing some great secret. "They've got a lot of billionaires in the group. If you'd like to learn more about them, they have a Wikipedia page and a website. The dig will start the last week of April. We're scheduled to leave Libya in early June, before the real heat sets in. But make no mistake, it will be hot there. We'll discuss preparations and how to fend off heat, dehydration, and fatigue at the orientation. I'm very much looking forward to this excavation, but my primary goal will be safety and health." He gave me a fatherly smile. "I've never lost a dig team member to illness or anything else and I don't intend to start now. Previous team members have called me Papa Paranoid."

I laughed. "How flattering."

Ethan glanced at his watch. "I've got a conference call in ten minutes." He got to his feet. "It's been lovely meeting you, and welcome to the team."

"Thank you! I still have so many questions." I got to my feet as well.

He picked my coat and hat off the quilt rack and handed them to me. "You can ask as many as you like at the team meeting, which will take place at Saltford High. We've been given access to one of the classrooms." He cocked his head. "Is that where you went to school?"

I shook my head. "No, I grew up on the other side of town. But I know where Saltford High is."

Ethan walked me to the foyer as I put my coat on.

"When is the meeting?" I asked.

"Tuesday evening at seven."

"Should I bring anything?"

"You might want a notebook for your own note taking, but I'll have a few handouts that will help. Otherwise, no. Just bring your keen self." Ethan tucked a hand into one of his pockets and opened the door. "I'll see you Tuesday. If you run into any issues before then, give me a call. I'll have some paperwork for you to sign when next we meet."

This was unbelievable. The dig of my dreams, handed to me on a silver platter. I didn't need my therapist's help or my boss's influence —it had just happened.

I knew there was more to it than that; I had been preparing for and working toward finding something like this for years. Still, up until a few days ago, prospects had been pretty bleak. And now, I could hardly believe my good fortune.

I jammed the hat on my head and gave Ethan a glimmering smile. "Sounds great. See you then!"

FOUR

I opened the doors to Saltford High and stepped through the foyer and into the large lobby. I had never set foot in this high school, as Beverly and I had lived on the far West side of town. I glanced at the pie-faced clock above the office doors. I was a few minutes early.

It was weird being back among the bricks of a high school. I wandered along trophy cases filled with glittering icons of achievement. I passed the list of honors students, their names framed in heavy oak and matted in a royal purple velour fabric. Beyond that were the photographs of the graduating students and the school photos of the younger grades. I walked slowly along the silent hall, taking in the smiling faces, the not so smiley faces, and the downright dour.

I paused before the image of a Japanese girl in grade eleven. There was something familiar about her. I scanned the name. Akiko Susumu. I didn't recognize the name, but I recognized the face. I squinted at her features, searching my memory. Surely this girl was the doppelganger of a girl who had been in her final year in my own high school when I'd been in grade nine. Grade nine students rarely made friends with graduating students. Her face had a compelling, ageless quality and a wisdom that seemed out of place on a student. I had never hung out with this girl or even said two words to her, but I knew her face.

Her countenance held me there for a long time. I wracked my brains for a reason she would be a grade eleven student at Saltford High after she'd already graduated from my high school. She had to have a doppelganger, or maybe an older sister who looked more like a twin.

The double doors squeaked open behind me and a young man came in, removing the sunglasses from his face. His gaze fell on me and he smiled, his white teeth stark in a tanned face. He had short dark curly hair and eyes the color of moss. He wore a green utility jacket, jeans, and white sneakers that had to be new. A single dull metal ring graced his right thumb and he carried a notebook under one arm.

"Hi, you must be here for the dig team kickoff." Australian accent. "I'm Jesse Tindall. I'll be one of the trench supervisors on our little excursion."

Jesse Tindall was far too cute to be an archaeologist, but I didn't say that out loud. I smiled back and took his hand. "Petra Kara. Nice to meet you."

"The meeting room is this way." He gestured for me to follow him. "We've used the room a few times before."

I fell into step beside him and we passed through a second set of doors and turned to make our way down a long tunnel lined with blue metal lockers. "You're an archaeology student?"

He bobbed his head. "Graduated from Australian National"—he put a brown hand over his heart—"known to us locals as ANU. What about you?"

"I haven't started my undergrad yet. I've been saving up. Next year."

Our footsteps echoed in the metallic hallway. "Any idea where you'd like to go?" He gave me a brilliant grin. "ANU is one of the best in the world."

"Top ten for sure." I smiled. Cambridge was widely acknowledged to be number one.

"We're in here." He gestured to an open door. A few voices could be heard in casual conversation.

It was a normal classroom, with a blackboard spanning one wall, a teacher's desk, and student desks. A projector hung from the ceiling and a whiteboard had been erected beside the teacher's desk. A map of North Africa had blossomed on the whiteboard, with Libya the only country outlined and speckled with names and markings. Several people turned to greet Jesse and me as we walked in.

A woman who looked as though she couldn't be much older than I was, with skin the color of cocoa and eyes the color of bronze, got up from her desk, smiling broadly. Before any of the three other people were on their feet she was crossing the room with her hand out. Her long black hair was up in a tight ponytail.

"Dig-mates!" Her words were laced with a British accent. "Welcome to the party. I'm Ibukun." She reached for my hand first and smiled warmly into my eyes. "Call me Ibby."

Everyone introduced themselves and I repeated every name as it was said, to help me remember.

Chris Brown, a short wiry fellow with red hair and glasses had joined from Ireland. He was studying at University of Toronto and in his second year. Sara Platt was an archaeologist originally from Vancouver but who had been digging in Portugal for the last few years. Sara was the area supervisor for the dig and Chris was another trench supervisor. A team of unskilled workers from Ghat would be meeting us at the site to do most of the dirty work. In the division of labor, I would also be part of this lowly group on the totem pole.

Ethan entered the classroom last, carrying a briefcase. "So, the Canadian contingent is all here." He shut the door behind him even though we were alone in the school.

Ibukun took a seat and patted the chair beside her, looking at me. I smiled and went to sit down beside her. "We might be the Canadian contingent," she said, "but I think only two of us are actually Canadian. You and Petra."

"True enough. We are international." Ethan plonked his briefcase on the teacher's desk and opened it, pulling out stacks of papers and rifling through them. "Here is the paperwork I'll need you each to go over, and there's a waiver at the back you'll need to sign. I'm required to walk through the risk factors with you." Ethan pulled a stack of pages from a briefcase and handed the stack to Chris, who was sitting nearest. Chris took one of the stapled sheets from the top of the stack and handed the rest to Sarah.

"Both the US and Canadian government have put out a travel advisory regarding Libya, warning tourists thinking of going there," he dropped his chin, "to change their minds. The advisory also warns those currently in Libya to leave as quickly as possible by the safest means possible."

"Doesn't apply to us though, does it?" Jesse added with a wolfish kind of grin, as he flipped through the documents.

"These advisories are necessary," Ethan said, "but I can assure you that there are and have been plenty of archaeological teams moving within and through Libya in the last year since the travel ban was lifted and the advisory changed to"—he made air quotes—"high risk. There are certain regions and cities within Libya that should absolutely be avoided, no doubt about it. But we'll be staying free from those of course and I'm happy to report we'll be granted twenty-four-hour security throughout the duration of the five-week dig."

"What is going on exactly?" asked Sarah. "I mean, I know there's been a civil war since 2014, but I don't know what it's about."

"I'll try to make a complicated matter simple." Ethan perched on the edge of the teacher's desk. "Basically there is a handful of rival groups who can't agree on who controls what territory in Libya. The three big players are the Libyan National Army, which by far controls the largest region." He grabbed the remote and pointed it at his computer. "Here, I'll show you."

The screen flashed over several images, many of which I guessed were of the dig site we'd be excavating, and landed on a multi-colored map of Libya.

A large pink blob covered the majority of the country from the eastern border and reached across the south and west. It was labeled *LNA*.

"The pink shows the Libyan National Army territory," explained Ethan, "which we won't be entering as we'll be flying into Tripoli." He pointed to a dot on the northwestern coast just at the edge of the next largest blob, which was green and marked with the letters *NA*. "Tripoli is in a region controlled by Libya Shield Force and The Government of National Accord, who know we're coming."

My eyes had already journeyed down into the yellow blob occupying the mid-west border and marked by a *T*.

"The yellow is controlled by Tuareg militants?" I guessed. I had done some research before coming to the meeting and knew that the Tuaregs were powerful in certain areas in Libya. They were the only main group Ethan hadn't mentioned yet.

"That's right. We'll be flying from Tripoli to Alawenat, where we'll meet our security team and Ibrahim Al Futuri, our connection at Libyan Antiquities, before journeying on by car into the Acacus. We have informed the Emergency Watch and Response Center in Ottawa in case the need for emergency assistance should arise. But, we've had a team there for a month already and they tell me they've had naps more exciting, and haven't seen a soul. So, I expect the same." He clapped his hands and rubbed them with visible glee. "Now that the safety obligations are out of the way, let's discuss the objective of the dig. I've already informed you how the site was first discovered by a paleontologist."

I felt eyes on me while Ethan was speaking and tried to ignore the feeling. This was my first real Old World dig. I clenched my pen tightly and attempted to push the feeling of being watched into the background.

"A sandstorm," Ethan continued, "blew into the area where the paleontologist was working. After the storm passed, he pulled up satellite images of the territory he was excavating and discovered large geometric anomalies near the caves that could only have been manmade. He notified the authorities, who sent in a team to do test pits. A water source and further humans remains were discovered along with definitive wall remains." Ethan put a hand over his chest. "I believe we are dealing with a new type of settlement or ritual structure."

As Ethan went on about the objectives of the dig, I was having more and more difficulty keeping my mind locked off from those of others in the room. A soft line of perspiration had formed at my brow and I wiped my hand across my forehead. I used my notebook to fan my face. My cheeks felt hot and flushed. I shifted uncomfortably in my seat and took a few deep breaths, letting them out slowly. Breathing exercises were one of the few armoring tactics I had, and when they failed, that's when foreign thoughts began to leak in my head.

"Now, onto a few more logistics." Ethan shuffled through his stack of paperwork and retrieved a sheet with a list on it. "Let's discuss how to pack properly, since we have a few rookies with us and let's face it, heatstroke isn't fun and neither is getting stuck out in the desert in a sandstorm, so!" He clapped his hands again and grabbed another stack of paper from the desk. He handed them to Chris, who took one and passed it on. "Let's go over a list of things you should pack, as well as precautions that should be taken. Shall we?"

The feeling of someone, perhaps more than one someone, being incredibly conscious of me had only grown. The little hairs on my upper back were standing on end. Cautiously, I lifted the gate on my mind and let thoughts and images emanating from dig-mates behind me into my mind.

Two thoughts from two different sources struck me hard, and confusion went off in my mind like fireworks.

From Ibby: *She's so young, and she seems like a nice girl. Why are they doing this to her?*

Jesse's thoughts floated into my mind like music drifting on the wind, much softer and less concrete, but the gist of it was that he thought I was one of the more beautiful girls he had ever seen. In spite of the loveliness of the sentiment, the whole feeling was dripping with sadness.

My head gave a throb and I dropped the gate down and closed my eyes to collect myself. What did Ibby's thoughts mean? 'Doing this to me?' Sending me on a difficult dig in the desert? I *wanted* to do it. I was *excited* to do it. I shook off my confusion. Picking up on thoughts was dangerous, and I immediately regretted that I had done it. And why was Jesse so sad while thinking I was beautiful?

My fingers trembled and I clenched the pen in my hand more tightly. I thought Jesse was beautiful too, but this was also dangerous. Getting close to people only resulted in getting hurt. People moved away, they changed, they sought out other relationships when they tired of you...and sometimes they died. Hadn't I already learned this in my young life?

With a mental shove that was almost violent in its intensity, I barred up thoughts from everyone else in the room. I needed to focus. One of Beverly's favorite snippets of wisdom came back to me. *What other people think of you is none of your business.*

FIVE

Goosebumps marbled my flesh as the plane banked over the Alawenat airport. If the moon had a landing strip for passenger planes, the Alawenat airport would be a good model for it. Only two runways and a cluster of colorless buildings sat in the gray sand of the western Sahara like a tattoo on the land. A small parking lot and arrivals building appeared in my window below, encrusted with bushes of green which were no doubt tended to with the utmost care.

Jesse peered over my shoulder and I pressed back into my seat to give him a better view.

"Not much to look at," Jesse said with a smile. He rubbed his hands together and caught me with a wink. "Now we've gone and done it. We're in the Sahara proper now, no turning back."

"Not that we'd want to," I replied, tightening my seatbelt as the plane straightened and dropped its nose to come in for a landing.

"Ah, I don't know," Jesse replied. "Scorpions, blasting sand storms, baking heat, camel spiders, no water for thousands of miles. I'm from Australia, I'm more used to that stuff than you are, little Canadian," he teased, bumping his shoulder against mine. "Tough desert conditions have a way of separating the women from the girls if you know what I mean."

I was about to elbow him and make a witty joke, but my mind had caught on a little hook called phobia. "Camel spiders?" I barely noticed when the wheel of the plane bumped down and the plane began to taxi to the airport.

Jesse's face brightened like a little boy who'd discovered the ticklish spot of a little girl. Hours of gleeful torture ahead. "Never heard of those, have you?" His tone took on that of a professor doing a very important lecture. "Now, camel spiders are a unique member of the class of Arachnida because technically," he held up a finger, "they are neither spiders nor scorpions. It just so happens, as I have been making a study of said Solifugae and have here for reference, a photograph." He fished his phone from his pocket, turned it on, and opened his photos and began to scroll.

"That really won't be necessary," I said, but found myself peering at his phone in spite of myself.

He turned the phone toward me.

"Ugh!" I immediately regretted looking, but also couldn't look away. "You're horrible!"

The photo showed a close up shot of a sand-colored arachnid which appeared to have five sets of legs and was equipped with pinching jaws so large in proportion to its body that they couldn't possibly be real.

"Please tell me that's photoshopped," I said weakly.

"Course not," Jesse replied, affronted.

"It can't be an arachnid; it has ten legs."

"That's a deception," Jesse said, lowering his voice to add drama. "What appears to be five sets of legs is actually four sets of legs"—he paused—"and one set of pedipalps."

"Pediwhat?"

"They're sensors, for detecting prey and for fighting. They're actually more like arms than legs because they never touch the ground."

I shuddered. "But these spiders are tiny, right?"

"Are you kidding me? These guys come in eensy to jumbo to burn-the-house-down, and yes those are official technical terms. But the kicker is two-fold." He held up a finger. "One, they hate direct sunlight." A second finger joined the first. "And two, they can run upwards of sixteen kilometers an hour."

I pushed the phone away and rolled my eyes. "Stop."

He put his hand over his heart. "I tell you this for your own good. Because if one day you happen to be digging in the sand or standing and throwing a nice dark shadow, and one of these monsters comes running straight at you, *don't run away*. If you do, it'll chase your shadow. Can you imagine running across the dunes of the Sahara with one of these chasing after you?"

"You are a horrible person," I said, unbuckling my seatbelt. "If you're done trying to terrify me, I do believe we have arrived."

"Oh," Jesse looked around as though he'd forgotten where we were. "Excellent." He tucked his phone away. "Don't say Uncle Jesse never warned you."

"Uncle Jesse?" I raised my brows.

His brown eyes met my gray, and a dimple appeared in his cheek. His eyes dropped to my lips, just for a second. "Yeah, you're right, that's really creepy. My bad."

"Sure is."

"Never happen again, I swear." He got out of his seat and popped the overhead bin open. He pulled out my bags first and set them on the seat beside me before pulling out his own. He bent and peered out the window at the desert dunes and skyline that appeared to reach out for an eternity. "Got your scarf?" he asked, all joking dispensed with.

I unzipped my backpack and pulled out a scarf I'd brought to cover my hair with. I shook it out and draped it over my head, tucking the edges the way I had learned from a YouTube video.

The wind was kicking up, and sprays of sand could be heard hitting the windows of the plane. I put my sunglasses on as I disembarked, still blinking against the glare as we walked across the white-topped concrete to the small airport building. A small truck pulling a trolley for luggage passed us going the other direction and pulled up alongside our plane. The air was much hotter than it had been in Tripoli, and even though the pavement was nearly white, heat waves still rose up from it and cooked us from the underside just as much as the sun did from overhead.

Stepping past the welcoming arches of the airport lobby elicited several sighs of relief from the dig team.

"Thank God they have air conditioning," Ethan sighed, taking his hat off and wiping his brow.

"There won't be air conditioning in the desert," replied Ibukun, taking off her sunglasses and peering around with her strange, bronze-colored eyes. "May as well get used to it now."

"I'll take air-con whenever I can get it," added Chris, craning his neck for the antiquities officer who was scheduled to meet us. "There is Mr. Al Futuri," he said, pointing discreetly at a man in a tailored white suit standing beside another man holding an iPad up with *Ethan Rich & Co* displayed on the screen. A small logo in the top right corner drew my eye, but it was too small to make out.

Ethan shook hands with the smartly dressed man, who removed his mirrored sunglasses and smiled. His eyes crinkled pleasantly and his gaze passed over all of us, hovering on me momentarily.

"Welcome to Alawenat," he said, speaking to all of us. "My name is Ibrahim Al Futuri. It's my honor to meet you. Antiquities is excited that you are here and is looking forward to the fruits our partnership shall yield over the next several weeks." He tucked his sunglasses into his coat pocket. "If you'll follow me, I'll introduce you to your security team, courtesy of the Libyan Archaeological Authority. They'll remain with you until you return to Alawenat for your flight home, so I hope you can get comfortable with each other."

We crossed the foyer and followed Ibrahim down a hallway to a large windowed entrance where a cluster of four men in khakis and fatigues sat chatting and laughing around a coffee table covered in water bottles and fatigue-colored satchels and bags.

When they saw us approach, they all stood up and their faces became serious. Four sets of keenly intelligent dark brown eyes took us in.

Ibrahim introduced them as Omar, Abu, Mifta, and Hassan. Each of them nodded politely as they were introduced and Mifta even gave us a glimpse of gleaming white teeth with a half-smile. Ibrahim spoke to the men in a language that Ethan had told us was called Tamahaq, a dialect local to Southeastern Libya. The men listened and nodded as Ibrahim pointed us out and gave them our names.

"Mifta here," said Ibrahim, putting a hand on the tallest man's shoulder, "has sufficient English and will be your translator for the duration of the dig. He will also be Head of Security." He nodded deferentially to Ethan and added, "With the understanding that you are the authority on the project."

Ethan nodded and addressed all four of our new security guards. "Thank you for taking on this work. Aman. Aman."

"If you'll follow Hassan to the vehicles, I believe they've already been loaded with your bags." Ibrahim gestured in the direction of the front doors.

The security team were on their way toward the airport lobby and front doors before Ibrahim had even completed his sentence, and we scrambled to follow them.

I was last in line and as we passed through the doors, and the hairs on my neck rose and turned to hackles. I looked behind me but there was nothing amiss that I could see.

"You okay?" Jesse was holding the door open and waiting for me.

"Yeah, fine." But as I turned back, a man standing on the second floor and looking over the balcony caught my eye. His eyes blazed in my direction, and the look on his face seemed to be full of warning. We made eye contact and for a moment I forgot to breathe. Slowly, his movement full of intention, he raised his right hand and placed the back of his wrist on his forehead. A thin tattoo was visible on the flesh just below his wrist. I squinted, but could make out only a simple line with a soft curve in the middle of it, like a primitive closed eye.

"Jesse?" I said, looking to see if he was still there. "Do you see—?" But when I looked back at the balcony, the man was gone.

"What?" Jesse came back inside to stand beside me and looked up at the vacant balcony.

I swallowed, looking from one end of the second floor hallway to the other, but there was no sign of the man. "Nothing, I guess."

"Come on." Jesse threw an arm around my shoulders. "Old dusty stuff awaits your paintbrush."

BETWEEN THE DIG TEAM MEMBERS, security, and our supply truck, our caravan came to four vehicles, all of them white and general purpose with big knobby tires for driving in the desert. The Alawenat airport was in the middle of nowhere in the desert, about thirty kilometers from the city.

Ethan rode shotgun in my vehicle, with Ibrahim at the wheel, who would stay with us only until we arrived in the city of Alawenat and would then give us a short tour before we dropped him back at the antiquities office and carried on to the dig site.

Jesse and I rode in the back seat. The rest of our team was broken up and mixed with the security team members.

My face was glued to the window as the desert stretched out on either side of us for what seemed like forever. The highway was narrow and unnamed. This was as remote as I had ever been in my life. As we continued south, the highway swung gently to the east. A tall dark line of cliffs on the east side appeared on the horizon as we got closer to Alawenat. The sun blazed down from a bright bluebird sky and not a cloud marred the color. A gentle southern wind made Ibrahim close the vents in the car to keep the sand from entering the vehicle. We passed two travelers swaddled in robes and turbans, two camels on leads strolling behind them. The camels were loaded up with lumpy sacks. It was hard to imagine where these travelers had come from and where they lived. They were smack in the middle of inhospitable desert terrain. I craned my neck to stare at them as the vehicles passed them by. One of the travelers lifted a hand in greeting and I waved back at him.

"There is the Acacus mountain range," said Ibrahim in his rich Tripolian accent. He pointed to the east where the wall of shadow put an end to the sand dunes. "That is where you'll be headed when we part. The highway that takes you south of Alawenat is good for about half an hour." He peered back at me briefly from the front seat as the empty desert flew by. "Then, you'll be going off-road and things can get a little bumpy. But the guys have already plotted out the journey so you're in good hands."

"Thank God for that," said Ethan, his fist gripping the handle above the door, his knuckles white.

I gave Jesse a smile and he winked back at me. If this empty, straight, paved highway made Ethan nervous, what was he going to be like once we headed off across the mountainous desert?

The city of Alawenat appeared on the horizon and I tried hard not to put my gaping mug between the front seats to stare.

"Wow," said Jesse, ogling from the other side of the vehicle.

"Beautiful, isn't it?" Ibrahim asked.

"It's an archaeologist's dream," I said.

"I'm glad you appreciate our rugged, remote city," said Ibrahim, slowing a little as the vehicle approached city limits.

It was difficult not to appreciate the beauty of Alawenat. Scuds of shrubs and bursts of palm trees speckled the city with green. The verdant shades against the taupes, browns, and beiges of the sand and architecture were a soothing pleasure to the eyes.

I gasped. "What is that?"

There was no need to point. A sand-colored castle perched up high on a rock thrust itself up and dominated the rest of the city. It was stark and intimidating in its beauty.

"That is the fortress of Alawenat," explained Ibrahim. He

waggled his head side to side and flashed a smile back at me. "It is not so old as you might like. The Turks began to construct it in the early twentieth century, but they didn't finish it. It became a stronghold for the Tuareg federation until the first world war, then the Italians took it over and finished it. In the second world war it was occupied by the French. You see, all of the world would like a piece of our beauty." Ibrahim chuckled at his own joke; most of the world didn't even know Alawenat existed. "So, we became independent in 1952 and since then," he gestured to the beautiful castle on a hill, "it is a tourist attraction."

"Is tourism big here?" asked Jesse. It was a fair question.

"Ha!" Ibrahim gave a laugh. "Most governments warn their people to stay away, so we do not see so many Westerners, except for historians and archaeologists—they will never stay away. There is too much to learn from our sands. But we get some of the more adventurous, let's say, local tourists. From Egypt, some from Europe, from Tunisia."

As we entered the city proper, I had a difficult time keeping my mouth closed. Beautiful sand-colored constructions with soft edges, arched terraces and walkways, elegant short towers and turrets were staged against the desert backdrop and encrusted with palms. The muted colors contrasted with the sky so beautifully that I took my phone out and began snapping pictures through the glass.

"You can roll your window down," said Ibrahim. "If you prefer, I can also stop at the old city, just for a short time."

"That would be amazing," I replied. "Thank you."

When the car stopped at a parking lot overlooking the old city and we stood gazing down into the old narrow streets, the passageways closed in by narrow white and beige rock walls that towered high above the people wandering through them, I had to fight to keep my emotions under control. Alawenat was a stop on our journey, but I could easily have spent weeks here wandering these streets and visiting and studying the prehistoric circular graves, walking the nearly deserted streets of the old city, and learning about the Berber way of life.

All too soon we were rounded up and back in the vehicles, heading for the small antiquities office which was Ibrahim's workplace for part of the year when he wasn't in Tripoli.

Ibrahim pulled up to a terracotta colored building with tall windows and squat palm trees lining a dirt walkway leading up to a porch.

"This is where I leave you," said Ibrahim. "You are in good hands with Mifta and the team." He looked at Ethan. "You can reach me with the satellite phone if anything is needed. And I know you have been told how to prepare for the sudden winds that can sometimes surprise us out of a still day at this time of year."

"Yes. Thank you for everything." Ethan and Ibrahim shook hands. "We shall see you in five weeks."

We inherited Mifta as our driver, and before the sun had yet crested in the sky, we were motoring south toward the Tadrart Acacus.

PAVEMENT BECAME HARD-PACKED DIRT, dirt became yellow dust, and yellow dust became thick golden sand. The sound of the tires softened, but I was amazed at how easy the desert was to drive on. Our drivers slowed by half as rocky chunks of basalt appeared on the undulating landscape, growing ever larger and closer together. Soon we were weaving our way among jutting flat-topped mountains rising straight up from piles of broken boulders and rubble clustered around the bottoms.

The first time going down a steep dune was heart-stopping. Mifta locked the brakes and we slid forward, our tires half buried in the runnels of sand carved out by vehicles passing this way before us. Each time we went down a dune, Mifta would unlock the brakes as the dune leveled out and we'd continue on. Our path through the

Acacus mountain range became narrow and serpentine, with walls of rock dappled with black basalt rising on either side.

Sometimes we would have to take a run at a dune, and Mifta would gun the Jeep across the flat hard-packed desert floor. Then we'd hit the sandy surface with a bump and we'd cross our fingers that the wheels would bite and hold until we made it to the top. We foundered only once in the sand, but with a push from Jesse, Ethan, and myself, the Jeep was free in minutes and we were back on our way.

We stopped for bathroom breaks and a stretch, parking in the shadow of a large overhang. The rock formations became more dramatic and beautiful the deeper we went. Huge natural arches and monoliths balancing on impossibly thin bases welcomed us. We saw wild camels wandering amidst scrubby grasses, looking like they knew exactly where they were going. One of them was so fluffy and white we joked that she was a camel/sheep cross.

"Did I hear someone brought ski gear?" Jesse asked Ethan from the back seat after Hassan remarked we were nearly there. Only one more hour to go.

Ethan looked over his shoulder and smiled at Jesse. "Where did you hear that crazy rumor?"

"Ibby may have mentioned seeing a ski-pole fall out of the supplies truck while you were poking around in there."

"Ski gear?" I laughed. "Does that work here?"

"Works very well," said Jesse. "Am I right, Mifta?" Jesse smacked our driver on the shoulder.

"Dune skiing very much fun," said Mifta nodding. He looked over at Ethan and back on the road ahead. "I thought this was serious work job, not fun making time."

"If you must know," replied Ethan with a mock serious expression, "I'm not all supreme intelligence and achievement, I'm also a very fun guy. It was going to be a surprise, kind of an ice-breaker activity for a day off. But I see my cover is blown." He smacked Jesse's hand.

"It's not blown," said Jesse. "Well, okay, it's partially blown. But only those of us in this vehicle know about it."

"And Ibby," I added.

"Right. And Ibby."

"But it'll be a fun surprise for everyone else. How many pairs of skis did you bring?"

"Only four, it's all we had room for."

"Two is all it takes to have a good time," Jesse grinned at me, white teeth gleaming in a Cheshire cat grin.

I smacked him on the shoulder.

"What?" He shrugged in mock innocence.

"We're here," said Mifta. "Almost." He lifted a finger from the steering wheel to point straight ahead. "You see that tall stone up ahead? It marks the last turn before the site."

Through the windshield loomed a tall slender finger of stone. Its top was heavy and like some I had seen before it, seemed to balance on far too small of a base.

"Do those things ever fall over?"

"Of course," said Mifta with a laugh. "What do you think all the rubble comes from?"

The caravan turned north, skirting the monolith and heading into a narrow curving path leading deeper into a more open area. The vehicles pulled into a shaded area not far from several canvas tents.

"Awesome." Jesse said. "Most of the boring work is already done." Several aluminum-framed canvas tents the same color as the sand had been erected in a haphazard semicircle. Another larger tent with its canvas rolled back showed picnic tables behind a screen of fine mosquito netting. There were no actual mosquitoes so I guessed the netting was more to minimize sand blowing into our food.

"When did the team before us leave?" I asked Ethan as the vehicle came to a stop.

"Just yesterday. But Sandy and Tarrin are still here."

"Who are they?" I unsnapped my seatbelt and opened the door, stepping out into the dry desert air and looking around.

"Tarrin is a researcher from Boston. She and Sandy are married. Sandy operates our GPR, and he's also a heck of a cook." Ethan got out and stretched his back.

"Petra, check this out!" Jesse called from where he and Ibby were studying something on the golden stone face. I crossed the packed desert floor, so flat it seemed someone had raked it with a machine. Small black pebbles jabbed at my feet through the soles of my shoes.

On the stone wall were drawings of land animals. Giraffes, cattle, a rhino, and even a crocodile. "Wow," I said, bending to take a closer look at the rock art.

"Hard to imagine this area covered in vegetation and wild animals," said Ibby, peering over the tops of her sunglasses at one of the giraffes.

"Are these the drawings that Ethan was talking about? The newly discovered ones?"

"Those are further in there." Jesse pointed to a narrow crack in the tall rock behind the vehicles. "They depict people in clothing and head scarves."

"There's also a hunting scene," added Ibby.

Gooseflesh rippled over my arms as I gazed at the drawings put there around three thousand BCE. "What a spectacular record of human history and culture, predating ancient Egypt."

Ibby and Jesse looked at each other. "Yes," Jesse said to Ibby. "She is a geek. I told you."

I flushed. "Aren't we all geeks? Isn't that why we're here?"

Jesse shrugged. "Saharan rock-art is cool, but have you seen Australia's aboriginal art?" He swiped a hand through the air. "Blows this stuff away."

"I doubt that," I said, crossing my arms.

"No, really." Jesse took out his phone. "Check this out." He came to stand next to me, his shoulder pressing against mine. He flipped through a few photographs and settled on one. "Get a load of that." He held the phone out for me to see.

The painting was downright spooky. Multiple alien-like faces of different sizes all clustered together, just their heads and shoulders visible. They had large, dark eyes with thick eyelashes going all the way around, and strange bulbous noses hanging overtop of where the mouths should be. "Where is this?"

"In the Wunnamurra Gorge. Western Australia. Aren't they incredible?" He peered over my shoulder at the photo, his face so close to mine I could feel his heat.

"Did you take this photo? I thought photographs of ancient cave paintings was forbidden without special permission?"

"I didn't take it," said Jesse. "It's just a screenshot from a website."

I handed the phone back to him. "Looks like it's worth a visit."

"Trust me, it is. You might never leave if you go to Australia." He put a hand over his heart. "You should come one day, as my guest."

"Maybe I will," I said, batting my eyes.

Ibby laughed and I jumped. I had forgotten she was even there. "Quit flirting, you two. Let's go check out the excavation site." She left the shadow of the rock wall and headed toward the campsite. Jesse and I shared a pink-cheeked smile and followed her.

SIX

The previous team had sectioned off multiple one meter by one meter excavation sites by pounding thick aluminum pegs into the ground and encircling the perimeter with rope. They'd also cordoned off a handful of larger trenches. Several inches of top layer had been removed and a few red flags inserted to mark anomalies and points of interest.

One of those huge monoliths of stone towered over one of the larger squared off test pits, casting it in a long lumpy shadow. The skinny pedestal the monolith balanced upon reminded me of a giant sledgehammer with a toothpick for a handle.

Ethan called out from a table he'd set up in the shade. "Can I have everyone here please?" Ethan had his fingers tented over a large hand-drawn map of the site.

A half-dozen laborers appeared from tents and materialized from behind rocks as Jesse, Sara, Ibby and I clustered around Ethan's makeshift podium. Smiles were exchanged, and hands shaken as we met our dig-mates.

"I'd like to take a moment to discuss division of labor, our grid, and stratigraphic levels." He pointed at the nearest test pit. "Most of these pits are set up for one worker, but as you can see there are a handful of larger trenches which can be worked over in pairs. We've line-leveled the string perimeters," he raised a finger, "which I must reinforce cannot be moved or shifted for the duration of the dig. These grids have been started from a datum point with a fixed GPS location. Please don't mess them up."

He lifted the map high so everyone could see it. "You are welcome to reference the map at any time. Each test pit also has its own grid. The pits have been given names and I have assigned you each to one. You're welcome to switch with each other if you wish; just be sure to tell me where you are at all times as I keep track of who is digging where. My goal is to have you remove twenty-five centimeters at a time. You'll find buckets and tools in the storage tent and in the back of the white van. Please," he put his hands together, "take care of your tools. It's not like we have a Wal-Mart around the corner if something breaks."

Ethan drew our attention to several tables under two large awnings. "Every find needs to be bagged. Deposit finds and frag-ments on the tables. Each stratigraphic layer gets its own bag. Put the site name, your name, and the trench number on each bag. We'll have hundreds of these bags before this dig is through, so please be diligent and do not forget to do this. Your trench supervisor can help you."

Ethan invited us to reference the maps and ask any questions. "Take your time, people." Ethan said over the mumble as we talked among ourselves and located our names and our assigned trenches and pits. "There is no going back once a find has been disturbed." He raised his voice higher. "Don't forget to wear a face mask at all times when digging. You'll find them in a box in the back of the van. Label yours so you don't get them mixed up. We only have so many so don't lose them."

I located my name on the map. I had been assigned to a trench called 'Dorn.' I smiled at the name. Someone was a *Game of Thrones* fan. I went to the box to retrieve some tools from the back of the van.

Ibby opened the passenger door of the nearby Jeep and I looked up to see a rock fall from the bottom of her shorts and onto the sand.

"You dropped something, Ibby."

She backed out of the Jeep and looked down as I picked up the stone. "Hell's teeth," she cursed. "I forgot to fix my pocket." She put a hand inside her pocket and turned it inside out, poking her finger through the hole.

"I brought a sewing kit," I said, admiring the nearly transparent yellow-green stone in the sunlight.

"You're a brick. I'd forget my head if it wasn't attached."

"What is this?" I held up the rock.

"It's Libyan gold tektite. Desert glass," Ibby replied. "Isn't it beautiful?"

I agreed. Turning it over in my palm, I admired how the sun illuminated a multi-colored palette of yellows and soft greens. "Did you find it here?"

"Yes, over by those petroglyphs. I was surprised to find it, actually; most desert glass is found much closer to the Egyptian border." She watched me turn the stone with my fingertips. "It's supposed to be twenty-eight million years old. It was used to make tools in the Pleistocene era, and it's also found in the jewelry of the Pharaohs."

What she said triggered the memory of an image I had seen once of a scarab beetle pendant. The beetle's body had been fashioned from a bright yellow stone. I nodded as I recalled it. "They called it the Rock of God."

I looked up at Ibby, who stood over me by a good three inches.

She grinned. "Exactly. So you've seen it before?"

"Not in person. Do you really think it's twenty-eight million years old?"

Ibby laughed and shrugged. "Who knows. They say a meteor of nuclear proportions landed in the desert, melting the sand into that." She jerked her chin at the tektite in my hand.

"Is it valuable?"

"Not really." She pointed to the stone with her pinky finger, the nail was buffed and painted with a clear polish. "This piece might go for sixty dollars or so but that's not why I picked it up."

"No?" I handed the stone back to her.

"No. I like rocks, gems, and metals. One could say I collect them, more to learn about their energetic qualities than their monetary value." She put her hand into the pocket that wasn't sitting turned inside out of her shorts. She pulled it out and opened her palm, showing a collection of three more baubles.

"Pretty." I peered at the glittery treasures in her palm. One stone was graphite gray but seemed filled with tiny crystals as it sparkled in the sun. The second was smooth and black as pitch. The third was also gray but had a blue and purple pearlescent quality completely unlike the first. "What are they?"

Ibby cocked her head inquisitively. "Is this really interesting to you? Don't get me wrong, I could talk about rocks all day, but my friends back in London have sworn they'd lock me in a box if I ever talk about my hobby in front of them again. This stuff is a snore to most."

"Everything is interesting when you take a closer look. Why do you think I like digging in the dirt?"

Ibby laughed. "Fair play."

"This one looks like obsidian." I pointed to the black shiny one.

"Yes, it's volcanic glass, you're right." She rubbed the stone with her thumb, cleaning away the dust and making it gleam. "This sparkly one is basalt."

"That's what these mountains look like on the inside?" I picked up the stone, observing how dull it was on the outside, and yet how spectacularly it glimmered in the light where a chunk had been broken away.

"Amazing, isn't it?" She pointed to the bizarre lumpy structures partially surrounding the excavation site. "I just grabbed this little guy from the rubble and smacked it with a hammer."

"And this one?"

"Ah, this..." Ibby picked up the pearly one with affection painted all over her face. Her eyes seemed to light up and reflect the opalescent coloring. "This is wolfram, but you might better recognize it by the name of tungsten."

"Tungsten?" I wracked my brains. "The stuff that lightbulb filaments are made of?"

She gave me a bored Garfield expression, eyelids at half-mast. "That's all you know about it?"

I winced with an apologetic grin. "Why, what's so special about it?"

"This little digit," she held the pearly rock under my nose, "is exceedingly rare, has the highest melting point of all the metals, the second highest boiling point, and is used in x-ray tubes and radiation shielding."

"Wow, you're a nerd, too" I said, laughing.

"You have no idea." She grinned.

"How do you know so much about rocks?"

Ibby closed the Jeep's door and followed me around to the back of the van, where we gathered tools, buckets, and face masks for excavating. "Some kids like dinosaurs, others like figure skating." She shrugged. "I liked rocks. I've been reading everything I could get my hands on since I was little."

"If you love them so much, why didn't you go into geology instead of archaeology?"

She looked thoughtful. "You know," she shut the van's doors, "that is a question I ask myself every day." She threw an arm around my shoulders. "Ready to get dirty?"

"I was born ready." And with that, my first North African excavation began in earnest.

SEVEN

The sun bore down on the excavation site, cooking our tools and baking us through our clothing. We were a week into our dig and I had finally mastered the art of the turban. Though I had a dark complexion which tanned well, I still put sunscreen on any bits of skin that the sun would find.

Jesse and I were alone in a larger trench called Camelot, where the original skull had been found. There was hope for more intact human remains. Where there were bones was where I wanted to be. Evidently, Jesse too.

Ethan and Ibby would both stop on their way by with their buckets of dirt, reminding us to drink and just saying hello. Excavating was painstakingly slow and patient work. Jesse and I talked and passed the job together. We filled our buckets and dry-screened the contents at the dry-screen station by sifting the dirt through a tray fashioned with a fine-mesh bottom. Then we bagged and labeled any finds and fragments and left them on the tables under the tent before going back for more.

The sifting station had been erected a considerable distance from the excavation site to prevent the mound of discarded dirt from blowing back into the site. There was a ton of walking back and forth for everyone.

I asked Jesse about his life in Australia, but it became a battle of who should be the focus of conversation as with every bit of information he'd give, he'd ask 'what about you' in return and then continue asking more and more questions. I had rarely met anyone more inquisitive about others, or more reluctant to talk about himself. Finally, I gave up on my efforts to keep the focus on him.

"You said you were raised in the foster system?" Jesse asked for the third time. "What was that like?"

"Not as bad as the movies like to make it look," I said. "Not for me, anyway. I had an amazing foster mom. Beverly." My heart gave a painful squeeze as I thought of her. "She was the best mother I ever could have asked for."

"Was?" Jesse's brows drew together.

"Cancer," I said. It still took my breath away how much power that one word could have. It could strike fear into the heart in less than a second, as it had mine the first time Beverly had said it to me. And, in this case, it was a loaded one-word answer that didn't require any more explaining.

"I'm sorry."

"Thanks."

"You never met your birth mother?" Jesse's face froze for a moment and his eyes looked hesitant above his face mask. "Sorry, is it okay to be asking you about this? I realize I ask a lot of questions. Not everyone likes it."

"It's all right." I dumped another scoop of dirt into my bucket. "I'm not sensitive about my past."

This wasn't entirely true. I didn't share my story with people because I didn't have any close friends. I had friendly acquaintances with schoolmates from high school and I was friendly with a few of my museum colleagues. Beyond that, I led a relatively solitary life. It wasn't that I liked being alone, because in fact I dreamed of having what Beverly had referred to in her old-fashioned way as a 'bosom buddy.' I sometimes found myself watching girls chattering away in a coffee shop, talking and laughing, their heads bent together. It looked lovely from the outside. But in my experience, these kinds of relationships always came to an end, usually painfully. Wasn't it better to avoid that pain altogether? Wasn't that pain worse than being lonely?

Noel and I had been over this territory many times during my years of therapy. Noel said I didn't let people in because I was fearful of being rejected or abandoned, and this was the same place my perfectionism and desire to be the best came from. This might be true on an unconscious level, but at the time it was difficult for a preteen to put a name to the reasons I pushed people away.

I had had people ask me in the past to talk about the circumstances of my birth. I usually just explained that my mother passed away when I was born and left it at that. The truth was a lot weirder. And somehow, for reasons I couldn't put my finger on, I *wanted* to talk about this with Jesse. The fact that I felt this way also made me a bit nervous.

"I only know what my therapist told me," I began, "which isn't really much to go on." I took a breath and adjusted my sunglasses. Sweat was gathering on my brow and under the nosepiece of my glasses. I took my glasses off and rubbed my face with my sleeve. I pulled my face mask away to let fresh air across my mouth.

"Here." Jesse handed me my water bottle. "I haven't seen you drink in a while." He reached for his own as well. He pulled his face mask down and took long swallows.

"Thanks." I took a drink, screwed the cap back on, and set it aside, then replaced my mask. "My mother was found lost and in labor on the streets of Saltford on New Year's Eve. Some kind strangers found her because they could hear sounds of distress and pain coming from behind their house."

Jesse had stopped digging and was listening, his eyes glued to my face. "She was all alone?"

I nodded. "They took her to the hospital. When they gave their report to the police, they said she was adamant that she didn't want to go, but she couldn't resist them while she was in labor. From the sounds of it, they had to force her into the back of their van and make her lie down."

"That sounds intense. Did your mother say why she didn't want to go to the hospital?"

"I'm sure she tried to," I sat up straight and stretched my back. It was difficult to find a position that wasn't uncomfortable after hours spent crouched or sitting in the dirt. "But she didn't speak any English and the couple who found her didn't know what language she was speaking. They found out later that it was Arabic."

"Wow! What was a pregnant lady who spoke no English doing wandering the freezing cold streets of a Canadian city? Was she homeless?"

"Apparently she was wearing expensive jewelry and clean clothing, so no. She was healthy and well-fed."

"Then what happened?"

"She died from eclampsia, but when I got older and couldn't stop asking questions, they also explained that she was very fearful. Stress can be very damaging during labor. It didn't help the situation."

"What was she afraid of?"

I shrugged. "They either don't know or they never told me."

Jesse frowned. "That must burn you up."

"What?"

"The fact that they might be withholding information from you."

"Oh." He was right, and that took me by surprise. I searched his eyes, which were full of second-hand anger. Warmth spread through my heart. He was furious on my behalf. "Yes, I have been upset about that. Nothing I can do about it though, aside from hack into their computer system to see anything in my files they've been withholding." I chuckled.

Jesse's face brightened as though this was a brilliant idea.

"I'm only joking." I laughed at the comical look on his face.

"Oh." His face actually fell with disappointment. "And what about your dad?"

"He's an even bigger mystery," I said. "I don't know a thing about him, not even his name. The janitor who understood a little bit of Arabic told the ER staff that my mother insisted there was no father."

"No father?" Jesse cocked an eyebrow. "Like an immaculate conception or something?"

I laughed again. "I think what she meant was that my father was not involved with her anymore."

"Oh." Jesse wiped across his brow with his hand, leaving a streak of dirt. A frown line appeared between his brows. "What kind of guy would knock up a girl and then leave her to fend for herself in a foreign country?"

"I try not to look at it that way." I reached up and brushing the dirt off Jesse's forehead.

"Thanks." He sat still while I cleaned him off, closing his eyes and leaning into my care. He cracked an eye open and pinned me with his dark green gaze. "How do you look at it then?"

"Who knows what happened? He could have died, or been detained somehow. I try not to assume the worst."

He cracked the other eye open and pulled back. "That's very generous of you."

"What good does it do me to demonize either of them?"

"Fair," he said. "Do you know your mother's name?"

I nodded and took another drink. "Her name was Tala Kara, she was an immigrant from Jordan. Apparently she wrote my name on a piece of paper only a few hours before she passed away."

"After the city?"

"I'm guessing so. She was Jordanian after all."

"Have you been there?"

"No, I have been so focused on saving money for university that I've barely been anywhere at all. One day, I will go to Petra. Of course." I glanced up at him. "Have you been there?"

"No," he said. "I've always wanted to. Maybe one day we can go together."

I blinked at him in surprise and my stomach gave a squeeze of anxiety. "Maybe," I said, quietly. I immediately stomped on the hope that sprang up like a burbling fountain. When people said things like this, more often than not they didn't mean it.

"Bollocks, blast and bloody hell!" came a frustrated cry on the wind. Jesse and I raised our heads above the hole.

"Sounded like Ethan," I said. "I think he's in the van."

We left our tools, climbed out of Camelot and made our way to the van which had its side door propped open. Sure enough, Ethan was sitting cross-legged on the floor of the van surrounded by equipment and holding a laptop in his lap. A tangle of cords surrounded him and a strange plastic gun-like tool sat at his hip. The panel on the gun's face was blinking with an error message.

Ethan's brow gleamed with sweat and large circles of damp stained his shirt at the armpits. A deep slash between his eyes and patchy red spots on his cheeks weren't the only tell-tale signs of his frustration. A manual had been ripped in half down the spine and the pages scattered across the floor of the van.

"Dude, your eyes are popping out on springs." Jesse leaned a shoulder against the van door. "Can I help?"

Ethan's eyes had a glassy, wild appearance. "I've been trying to pull the data from the handheld for the last half hour. Do you know anything about XRF technology? Oh, I don't even care." He handed the laptop to Jesse. "Please take this before I throw it."

"I don't, but..." Jesse perched on the running board of the van and steadied the laptop on his knee. "Let's take a look."

Ethan let out a long, hopeless sigh. He grabbed a kerchief and mopped his face. "Hand me that water there, would you please, Petra?"

I handed Ethan the bottle tucked into the netting of the seat back. "What's an XRF gun for?"

"It's a new-ish technology. At least to archaeology," Ethan explained, the red in his face slowly returning to a less alarming shade. "It saves us having to collect soil samples and send them to a lab." He tapped his finger on the tool at his hip. "It's like a Tricorder from Star Trek. It has the capability of quantifying and qualifying pretty much any material on earth."

Jesse's eyes flashed up. "I doubt she's a Trekkie, Ethan," he said. A dimple in his cheek appeared before he ducked his head back to the computer. He frowned and checked the cords linking the gun to the laptop. He picked up the gun and began to interact with the control panel.

"You never know." Ethan looked at me hopefully.

"Not a Trekkie. Sorry to disappoint," I replied. "What are you analyzing?" I put my own water bottle to my lips and took a big swig.

"Poop."

I turned my head just in time to spew the water all over the side of the van.

Ethan and Jesse both burst out laughing.

I mopped my wet face with my sleeve, laughing too. "Excuse me?"

"I'm serious," replied Ethan. "Chris came across a circular deposit in his trench with a speckled layer in the sand."

"Possible sign of an ancient bathroom," added Jesse, glancing up from the gun.

Ethan nodded. "They would dig a deep hole to do their business in but over time, the pit fills up with garbage and soil. Chris just found the circular pattern today and suspected it might be a latrine. The gun saves us oodles of time spent analysing soil samples." He frowned at the gun in Jesse's hand. "When it's working properly."

I gave Jesse a look. "So much for my pro con list."

"Your pro con list?"

"I made a list about the pros and cons of working in archaeology. One of the big pros was," I made air quotes, "has little to no contact with poop.'

Jesse chuckled. "Yeah, better switch that to a con." He handed the laptop back to Chris. "Here you go. Problem solved."

Ethan's face widened with surprise and relief. "Really?" He took the laptop and surveyed the screen.

"Yep. You just had the wrong COM port and the settings were messed up."

Ethan looked at Jesse like he was a god.

Jesse shrugged, looking uncomfortable. "I'm good with technology." His cheeks were tinged with pink.

"Obviously." Ethan settled in for the task at hand as Jesse and I turned away to go back to work. "Don't wander far, La Forge."

"La Forge?" I echoed to Jesse as we stepped down into the trench. "Another Star Trek reference?"

"I'm guessing yes," whispered Jesse. "I won't look it up in case it's unflattering." He stepped down into Camelot and I followed.

"I doubt it's unflattering." I smiled and picked up my trowel. "You made his problem go away like that." I snapped my fingers. "How did you figure it out so fast?"

Jesse's cheeks colored again. "It was nothing." He ducked his head. Something about his manner made me realize Jesse didn't want praise, and he didn't want to talk about it any further.

Seemed there was a lot he didn't want to talk about.

EIGHT

It was Sarah who first brushed the sand away to reveal human teeth—beautiful, straight, white, and still lodged in the jaw. We called the find Tafuri. The painstaking job of uncovering whatever was left of her was still ahead and had to happen quickly. Once bones were exposed to the elements, they began to deteriorate much more quickly. When I asked for the job of unearthing the rest of her, Sarah was happy to pass it over to me.

Slowly revealing her ribs, the bones in her hands and feet, and the knobs of her spine was an exercise in amazement for me. No matter how uncomfortable it was kneeling on the sand, crouching against the breeze, or lying flat on my belly with my chin resting on my arm, I never tired of it. It was not the case for my colleagues, for as I entered the second day of uncovering her, I was left there for hours on my own.

Ethan showed me how to check the sciatic notch of the pelvis. As it was wider than his thumb, it was a significant indicator that the remains were female.

"Do you see how small her supra orbital bones are?" Ethan pointed with his pinky at her brow. "And how small the mastoid process is?" He moved his pinky to the knobby bone behind where the ear would have been. "These point to a female."

I nodded, pulling my face mask down a bit so I could see better. "Her jaw is small and overall the skull is very round." I added. "It talks about that in the field manual."

Ethan nodded and though his mask was covering his mouth, I could tell he was smiling. "You've clearly chosen the right path for yourself, Petra. Keep up the good work. Would you like to help Sarah with the documentation?"

"I'd love to." I smiled back at our team leader, heart full. I felt closer to realizing my dream than I ever had in my life before. I was living as an archaeologist, and loving it.

Tafuri was drawn, photographed, and then wrapped up with brown paper and deposited into boxes to protect her.

We called the next skeleton Anwa, and I set to work uncovering it with the same care I had shown Tafuri. Even once the full skeleton had been uncovered and a second one discovered, no one seemed as magnetized to them as I was.

A hot and still afternoon found me lying on my stomach, using a paintbrush to pull sand away from Anwa. Sarah and I had started out the day working together, but as the sun climbed, Sarah complained of a headache and retreated to her tent for a rest.

After lunch, I was still digging alone. The sand on these bones tended to clump and stick more than it had on Tafuri's bones, and I needed something stronger than a brush. I cast about for another tool and spied a wooden pick—just what I needed. With a tummy full of lunch, I felt drowsy and slow. I could probably have used a nap myself before commencing the afternoon's work. I stretched my arm out for the pick, but it was just beyond my reach.

I glanced toward camp, where Hassan and Abu, two of the security guards, were drinking from tin cups, talking and laughing. No one else was in sight and Hassan's and Abu's backs were to me.

Locking my eyes on the pick, I gave the tool a mental pull. It slid toward me in the sand and I grabbed it. "Gotcha!" I discarded the brush in favor of the pick.

The sound of a boot on sandy rock made me gasp and look behind me.

Mifta was standing on top of some basalt rubble next to the pit. He was wearing reflective sunglasses. I couldn't tell where he was looking.

"Hello, Mifta. You made me jump. Didn't see you there."

Seconds passed before he answered and each moment of silence filled my stomach with dread. Had he seen what I had done? I cursed myself. Why hadn't I just gotten up and grabbed the tool like a normal person? Of all the stupid mistakes made for laziness.

"I apologize," said Mifta finally. "I'll make a little more noise next time I do a round." Was it my imagination, or did his tone seem flat and a little sarcastic?

I gave him a nervous smile but he didn't return it, possibly because I was still wearing my face mask so he couldn't see it. He stepped down from the rubble and walked by, his expression unreadable.

I was only left to hope that he hadn't observed my little stunt. I promised myself I wouldn't make such a stupid mistake again.

Mifta joined Hassan and Abu. He filled a cup with water and stood with them, drinking. I caught him looking back at me more than once. They spoke to each other, and the words drifted by on the wind. What were they conversing about?

Cautiously, I closed my eyes and lifted the gate between my mind and Mifta's, probing his thoughts for a clue. What I picked up was a stream of Tamahaq as he spoke with the men. The base of my skull throbbed and I shut the gate, rubbing the back of my neck. I frowned and watched their backs for a while. When they burst into laughter, I tried to relax. They wouldn't be laughing if Mifta had told them I'd moved a tool with my mind.

It was a good thing I was left to my own devices for the rest of the afternoon's work. I was far too distracted by worry to make decent conversation with anyone.

"EXCUSE ME!" Ethan tapped his knife against his plastic glass and stood up at breakfast the following Saturday. He put a hand over his heart. "I have a little surprise for you, my hard-working team, to celebrate the success of the dig thus far and as a reward for the excellent job you have all done over these last couple of weeks."

Jesse and I shared a look and Jesse winked. Someone turned on a stereo and the funky refrains of a famous Bee Gees song filled the tent. A head appeared in the doorway wearing goggles and a bright pink and teal eighties one-piece ski suit. A thick knit hat with a huge pompom on the top bounced as Ibby bobbed her head to the music.

The tent exploded in laughter and applause as Ibby began to strut back and forth, modelling the retro outfit and throwing her hips all over the place. A pair of vintage skis were propped over her shoulder and as she turned, they flew over Mifta's head. He ducked, laughing.

"My I present, sand-skiing in the Saharan desert," Ethan yelled over the din. He spread his arms wide and bowed with a toothy grin. "A once in a lifetime opportunity, ladies and gents. Let it never be said that Papa Paranoid was also boring."

Ibby ripped the toque off her head, sweat making her hair damp. "Brought to you by Speedstick's aluminum chlorohydrate anti-perspirant spray." She propped the skis against the tent wall and tugged the one-piece open at the neck, shimmying out of the top half. "The big guns of anti-stink. It'll kill ya, but at least you'll go down smelling pretty."

Jesse covered his mouth as he laughed. He leaned over and said in my ear, "Skiing down sand dunes. We're real rebels, the lot of us."

"I hope I didn't miss the party," said a feminine voice over the din. A tall, slender woman in a white fedora appeared in the doorway of the tent. She had long blond hair streaked with gray and tied back in a braid. Her tanned face was lined with years of experience. Her eyes were bright blue and radiated a keen intelligence.

"Molly, you made it!" Ethan went around the table. "I didn't even hear your vehicle pull up over these hooligans." Ethan and Molly gave each other a tight hug. Ethan turned to the rest of us. "This is an old—"

"Very old," the woman added, to laughter.

"Friend of mine from Uni days. Professor Metcalfe is a well-known fixture at Harvard—"

"Just call me Molly." A charming pink tinge dusted Molly's cheeks as she waved hello to everyone. "A little birdie told me there was going to be dune skiing here today. I hope I didn't miss it?"

There was a rustle of movement and clanking of plastic dishes and cutlery as the crew rushed through cleaning up after breakfast. Twenty minutes later, the entire team including the security men, were gathered at the top of a sand dune.

"We only have four pairs of skis and poles, so we'll have to take turns," Ethan shouted over the laughter and general silliness. It seemed everyone really needed a day off.

I wandered over to where Molly was applying sunscreen under the shadow of a rock shaped a bit like an Easter Island head.

"I'm Petra." I held out my hand.

"Nice to meet you." Molly shot me a sparkling smile from a face half coated in zinc. "You sound decidedly Canadian."

I laughed. "East Coast. You sound decidedly Bostonian."

"Guilty." She handed me her tube of zinc.

"No, thanks." I held up a hand. "I'm already greased up."

"You have that beautiful olive skin. You probably get as brown as a chocolate cookie."

I laughed. It was true. "I still try not to get too much sun."

"Smart." She rubbed the sunblock over the back of her neck and under her braid. "You'll avoid looking like a leather handbag. Like I do." She added more sunblock and coated the backs of her hands.

"Things I wish I had known when I was your age. I'm from the generation that used to roll in baby oil and then lie there with tin foil to magnify the frying effect. So dumb. I have to be extra careful now. I've already had melanoma once. That's a scary business."

"What brings you out into the desert? And where are you staying? It's like you popped up out of the sand." I gestured at the empty desert that spread out vacant for miles around us.

She belted a laugh. "Great question!" She slapped her hat back on her head and tossed her sunblock into the knit sack dangling from her shoulder. "I'm an anthropologist. I was given permission to study the ongoing conflict between tribal militants and the rival groups seeking control here, specifically in the southwest."

"Wow!" I fell into step with Molly as we made our way over to the group waiting for their turn to career wildly down hot desert sand. "How is that going?"

"It's not easy. I'm interested in how ethnicity affects the integrations of those displaced by political violence. I'm living in a Tuareg camp about a two-hour drive thataway." She pointed two fingers to the west. "They seem to tolerate my presence. Not all of them talk, but I respect that. These kinds of studies take time."

"Ethan let you know he'd be running an excavation not far away?" I asked.

Ibby walked by, handing out water bottles and we each took one.

Molly nodded and took a swig of her water. She leaned in close and said, "Truth be told, we were sweethearts many years ago. Turned out we were better friends than lovers–"

I blushed at this easy sharing of confidence on her part, not sure what to say.

"We never lost touch." Molly looked at me, and it felt as though her bright blue eyes were really taking me in. "He was one of those special ones, you know. One of the ones that never lets go of you, and you never let go of them?"

I opened my mouth, but was still lost for words. Actually, I didn't know. But I didn't want to contradict her. I made a sound that could be taken as an agreement, but changed the subject. "In your studies, have you come across anyone with a tattoo across the wrist? A curved line, like a closed eye?"

Her eyebrows shot up, and lines in her forehead sprang to life. "That's very specific. Across the wrist, you say?"

I nodded. "Maybe it doesn't have to be on the wrist, I don't know." I told her about the man at the airport, how he'd raised the back of his hand to his forehead and flashed the simple tattoo outward at me.

"Hmmm." Molly retrieved a notepad and pencil from her knit bag. "Can you draw it for me?"

"Sure." I took the pad and pencil. "It was very basic." I drew the shape for her. It looked as though a straight line had been pushed at by something round, creating a soft curve in the center.

"Oh. I do know this symbol," said Molly, taking the page from me. "Was it like this?" She laid it over her wrist so that the symbol ran up the inside of her wrist.

I nodded. "That's right. So it looked like a single closed eye when he held his hand up and his wrist out."

"Strange that he would do that to you. This symbol is meant to ward off intrusion of the mind."

My jaw slackened and I stared at her. My forearms prickled and even under the hot Saharan sun, a cold feeling swept over me. "Are you sure?"

"Yes, I believe so. There are many regional superstitions here." She tapped the page. "This is one of them. And, you are very astute. It is a closed eye."

"Who's next?" yelled Mifta as he crested the hill with the skis, pouring sweat and wearing a face-splitting grin. Hassan climbed up behind him.

"Shall we give this a whirl, then?" Molly put her hands together and rubbed them. "It's been a long time since I nearly broke my neck."

Molly and I strapped on the skis, the goggles, and the helmets. It was so hot inside the helmet I thought my brain was going to cook. She nodded at me as we pointed our tips downhill and I watched as she whooped and dug her poles into the sand, shooting down the dune and carving like she'd done it a thousand times before.

I was so bemused and distracted by what I had learned that I did a very poor job and fell twice, scraping my elbows and bruising my tailbone. By the time I got to the bottom, my heart was pounding and I felt like I'd been kicked in the backside. I tried to make the pizza shape with my skis to brake, ploughed up too much sand and flipped over on to my belly.

"Rode it like a champ," said a voice at my elbow. Jesse helped me up and brushed me off.

"I didn't ride it so much as it rode me," I replied, laughing and feeling a little shaky. I popped my feet out of the skis and began to unstrap the boots.

"Do you want to go again? I'll go down with you next time?" Jesse helped me out of the helmet and the fresh air against my cheeks felt delicious.

"Very funny." I handed the equipment to one of our laborers who was eyeballing them eagerly. "Please take these away before I kill myself. I do believe I have done enough dune skiing to last me a lifetime."

Jesse handed off the helmet and beckoned for me to follow him. "Cool, because there's something I want to show you."

NINE

I followed Jesse toward a cluster of low red rocks just beyond the ski area. He hopped over the tops of the rocks and then slowed, getting to his knees and then to his belly.

"What are you doing?"

He looked up at me and put a finger over his lips, beckoning me to lie down beside him.

I went to my belly and mimicked him as he army crawled to the edge of the rock and peered over. I shimmied up beside him and followed his gaze.

"Oh my!" I whispered.

There, in the shade of the rock, digging in the sand like he hadn't a care in the world, was a camel spider. I recognized it instantly from the photo Jesse had shown me before.

"Are you afraid?" Jesse whispered, looking at me with his brows drawn in concern. "I found him working here and thought it was so funny, because we were just talking about these on the plane."

I shook my head. "I'm not afraid." I was a little creeped out, but also admittedly fascinated. The creature was on the large side, as far as creepy-crawlies went, maybe three inches long. But he was a good two feet below us and seemed to be so preoccupied with what he was doing that he didn't even know he was being watched.

"Amazing. Right?" Jesse rested his chin on the back of his hands and gazed at the creature.

I agreed. The camel spider was pushing sand around at the mouth of a tiny hole, presumably his living quarters. He worked fast and efficiently, moving like he knew exactly what he was doing. It was mesmerizing to watch a living creature building himself a home with such focus and determination. In this way, he was not really terrifying at all, just a guy going about his daily grind.

"I think he's making a comfortable place for a mate," Jesse whispered, with a grin. "The arduous lengths we men go to for the right woman."

I chuckled. "I'm guessing you've never ripped all of your leg hair out at the roots, or suffered through an acid peel?"

"An acid..." He shot me a horrified look. "Is that a thing?"

"That and worse, so don't complain about the work men do to attract a mate."

He held my gaze without saying anything for so long that I blushed and had to look away. He tucked a lock of my hair behind my ear. Then he said, as naturally as saying 'please' or 'thank you,' "All *you* have to do is breathe."

My face heated at his familiar behaviour. I might have pulled away from someone else, but there was something in me that wanted to lean into his touch. *Jesse is a flirt*, I reminded myself. *This is what he's good at. It doesn't mean anything.*

The sound of laughter from the group back on the dunes washed over us and we turned to watch the party. Ethan and Molly were careening wildly down the dunes, on the edge of control. There was a long whooping sound from one of them as they raced for supremacy.

I couldn't help but laugh at the way the whole team was into the race, hollering and yelling and laughing with their hands cupped to their mouths, faces shining with sweat. I glanced over at Jesse but he was not laughing. Instead, his expression seemed serious, pensive, as he watched the merry-making.

"What's wrong?"

He shrugged. "Nothing."

We watched for a few more moments, sitting up straight and leaving the camel spider to his work.

"You know I was raised in Australia..." Jesse began.

My ears perked. He was finally going to share something personal with me? "Yeah?"

"Well, I traveled for a time when I was twenty. I spent some time on an island in Thailand, surfing, enjoying Thai food. I worked at a beach bar for a season, mixing drinks for locals and tourists." He lifted his hat, ruffled his hair and set the hat down again. The hair at his temples was damp with sweat and nearly black. "One night, late, just before closing, a woman came to the bar and ordered a cocktail. She was alone."

I made a sound that indicated I was listening.

"I served her, and I thought something was so familiar about her. It happens sometimes, right? Someone can ring a bell in your memory, even if you've never actually met them before."

"Sure." I was reminded of the photo of the Japanese girl on the wall of the Saltford Highschool lobby. I even remembered her name —Akiko.

"I watched her for a long time." He raised a defensive hand. "Not in a creepy way. Just in a stealth way I have."

"You're stealthy?"

"As a fox, when I want to be. I didn't want to make her feel like she was being observed, but man I watched her hard, trying to puzzle out where I knew her from. She was old, so it was even weird-er." He gave me a lopsided smile. "I don't hang out with so many old ladies."

I laughed. "I bet you don't."

"Anyhow, after she left, I went home. And I kid you not, I thought about it for weeks afterward. But it wasn't until I got home to

Australia and I ran into an outdated newspaper at the barber shop that I figured it out."

"Why? Who was she?"

"She was a soap star named Bernadette Peters."

"Never heard of her."

"No, you wouldn't have, she was a B-star, but she had a devoted following in OZ." He waved a hand. "Who she was is not important."

"No?" I didn't get it. "Wasn't her identity the point of the story?"

"No. The important part is that she had been reported dead of an overdose about a week before she walked into my bar."

"No way!"

Jesse nodded. "I kid you not. I even kept the newspaper clipping."

"Maybe it wasn't her? Maybe it was her doppelganger. They say we all have one."

"Maybe." Jesse shrugged. "But I don't think so. I'm very good with faces, and even better with gestures and body movements. Everyone has their own way of walking, their own way of moving their hands. I had grown up with her on the TV screen every weekday."

"You watched soaps when you were a kid?" I laughed. "I can't picture that."

Jesse smiled and shook his head. "They were always on in the background. My mom liked them. Bernadette was one of her favorite stars. She was really beautiful, in that made-up, soap-star way. She had these huge eyes, and this big bouffant blond hair, like yellow cotton-candy." He made a gesture with his hands to show me just how big the bouffant was.

Jesse smiled at the way I was laughing at him. His accent and facial expressions made his story even more entertaining.

"I would have recognized Bernadette if she'd had a sex-change." He held up a finger. "Which she hadn't. She looked different for sure, but I pegged her."

"So you think she faked her death?"

"Sure seems so to me." Jesse chuckled. "And I actually don't think it's that uncommon."

I gazed out at the party on the sand, thoughtful and still bemused about the story. A few faces were glancing over at us. Ibby spied us and beckoned us to come back to the group.

Jesse got to his feet and helped me up and we began to walk back over the stones to join the crew.

"Why did you tell me that story, Jesse?"

Jesse turned to face me and his expression was so serious that it brought me to a sudden standstill.

"I'm just saying that if you really look—" He squinted to emphasize his words. "If you pay attention and you really *watch*—" His mossy green eyes bored into mine with an intensity that made it impossible to look away. His voice was low, his words obviously for my ears only. "You'll see things that others wish to keep hidden. Most people are blind. Don't be one of them."

"Jesse." My heart seemed to squirm up into my throat.

But Jesse grabbed my hand and pulled me toward our dig-mates, a smile on his face, carefree.

Jesse's story, or more accurately, the attitude he'd implored me to take, haunted me for several days afterward. But as the weeks passed by, the excitement and tasks of the dig became my world.

I did watch. I watched as human remains, ancient cooking tools, and Neolithic weapons emerged from the Saharan earth, speaking to me straight from history louder anything else going on around me.

TEN

It wasn't the noise of the night that woke me, but rather the stillness. Lying there on my Therm-a-Rest, I went from a dead and silent sleep to wide awake. My eyes opened to blackness, my ears perked. There was no wind, no sand spattering against the sides of my tent, no whistle of air as it whispered through holes in the rocks around our camp. I blinked and rubbed my eyes, then sat up. I hugged my knees for a moment, listening to the remarkable stillness, the disconcerting lack of sound.

I found the headlamp in the pocket beside my bed and clicked it on, leaving it in its pouch so it wouldn't assault my eyes. The interior of my tent was cast in a green glow, the top of my open luggage illuminated while the bottom half remained swaddled in dark—like it was floating in a sea of soft black fabric. I fumbled for my hair elastic and raked my hair up into a haphazard ponytail. I pulled on a long-sleeved t-shirt, a pair of shorts, and yanked on my tri-shoes, chosen for the very reason that I could don them without bothering with laces. I unzipped my tent door, clicked off my headlamp, and crawled out into the night.

"Wow," I whispered, looking up. The sky arched above me like a massive inky dome, and millions of stars twinkled across it in clusters —their light stark and perfect against the backdrop of the universe. The moon was small and high in the sky, its light cold and blue and bright as a halogen headlight on a dark highway. A single cloud reached across the man in the moon's face, looking like fingers, as though he was checking to see if he needed to shave.

"The moon was a ghostly galleon, tossed upon cloudy seas," I murmured, not knowing why that particular piece of poetry had taken up permanent residence in my brain. Turning slow and taking in my surroundings, which now seemed completely alien to the world in which we operated in the daytime, the Acacus formed rough black shapes that blocked out the stars. They looked like the backs of gigantic grazing animals. I walked toward the cluster of rocks, the sturdy sand cushioning my steps. I wondered if this was what a ghost felt like as I passed through our camp and out the other side toward the rocks beyond. The air was dry and still and body temperature. It was the first time I felt completely comfortable and not vulnerable to some aspect of the Saharan environment.

I passed into the narrow funnel leading through the rocks, and the horizon narrowed into a strip of stars above me. Winding my way through the narrow rocks made me feel as though nature had built a labyrinth that was meant to be walked at night. I passed where I knew the drawing of the rhino was, the moon lighting my path. Just beyond, I knew where the rock formed natural steps, and I climbed the twelve feet or so to the top of the rock. There, I stopped. The only sound was of my breathing. The moonlight dusted the tops of the rocks with light and showed the winding serpentine tops and the black gulfs in between.

A sound of movement, like sand gritting against rock, made me gasp and look to my left. A small dark shape was silhouetted against the sky, a prone body with its head lifted seemed to turn to look at me.

"Petra?" A voice called softly.

My thumping heart calmed and I sighed with relief.

"Jesse?" I walked the tops of the rock, the moon showing me the way, to where he lay. I sank down beside him and sat cross-legged. "What are you doing up?"

The smell of his soap drifted to my nose, juniper and lemon.

"I could ask you the same question," he replied, sitting up. "I think it was the stillness that woke me."

"Me too." I looked up. "Isn't it breathtaking?"

"Yeah, it's awesome. How lucky are we? This is why we dig, right? You can put it on your pro con list."

"One of the reasons." I smiled in the dark.

The moon dusted Jesse's features with cool blue light. His cheekbones and lips stood out, his eyes glinting wetly.

We passed a few minutes in silence. I was captured by how the tops of these rocks, with the rivers of black shadow laced in between, looked like the pathways of desert spirits. They were the opposite of damp wooded trails closed in by foliage and tree trunks. These paths were embraced only by space on either side, and a misstep meant dropping into the dark land hidden between them. Ahead on the horizon jutted a tall elegant rock, one we'd taken to calling the dreaming spire.

"The rocks almost look like they make a trail of islands the way the moonlight falls on them," said Jesse.

"I was just thinking that same thing." Had that been accidental telepathy of some kind, I wondered. Or was it just chance that the rock formations struck us the same way?

"Let's run them," Jesse said, getting to his feet. He bent and held a hand down to me.

"Is it dangerous?"

"Not if we stay in the center. Come on, how often does one have the opportunity to run the tops of the Acacus mountains under a sky full of stars?"

"When you put it like that." I took his hand and let him help me to my feet. We came face to face, and it seemed the stars were moving and dancing in my periphery. For a breath I looked up at him and he looked down at me. His hands landed on my waist and he pulled me close, our chests and stomachs pressing together.

"Petra," he whispered.

"What?" He had my heart suddenly banging like a set of kettle-drums at the unexpected closeness.

"Are you ready?"

"Ready?" The question took me off guard. "What do you mean?" I was certain he was about to kiss me.

He released me. "Ready to run? I'm going that way."

I grinned. "I was born ready."

He chuckled. "I'll bet you were."

"See you at the dreaming spire, Oz." I took a flying leap off the top of our rock and followed the trail the moonlight showed me. I heard Jesse laugh and take his own flying leap across a channel of sand, landing in a run.

My runners gripped the uneven rock surface and I stayed on my toes as I scampered along the serpentine trails and rock islands, giggling. I could hear Jesse running and laughing, and see his silhouette bobbing against the starry backdrop as he followed his own trail. My breathing grew increasingly labored. It was like running on an alien planet. I could peer down into the spaces between the rocks, small drifts catching the light here and there. If I fell, I would have anywhere from an eight to a twelve foot drop, but at least it would be into sand. I pushed that thought from my head and kept my eyes trained on the path the moon unfolded before me. The landscape changed, with larger banks of sand reaching up and wrapping over the rock in sections. In some places it seemed as though nature had provided banks to climb up or slide down. The sound of grit under my feet increased, and my footfalls were no longer soundless.

I looked over at Jesse and when I couldn't find his shape right away I slowed, looking up and down alternately as I ran.

"Jesse?" I finally called. When no answer came, I slowed to a walk so I could scan the rock tops better. I took a deep breath to feed my working muscles. "Jesse?"

My foot slid on grit and my right leg, the one whose turn it was to take my weight, swept off the rock and to the side. I gave a little shriek as the foundation beneath me began to move and run. Sand shifted and drained into some world beneath me that I couldn't see.

I gasped, struggling for purchase. But there was no solid rock to catch me, and I fell. My hip bumped and scraped against stone as the sand drained away beneath me and I went with it, now screaming in earnest. I was swallowed by a black maw and sliding. I had no perception of how fast I was moving because the dark gave up no secrets.

Fingers of fear closed tight around my throat and guts, squeezing with cold intensity. Sand flew up, half-filling my mouth. I covered my face with my hands as I slid in a trough of sand, half-expecting to be stabbed and scraped by rock at any moment.

I landed painfully on my knees, then fell to my hip and onto my hands. Sand filled my hair, my face, my clothes, my shoes. I coughed and spat the grit from my mouth. My heart thudded like the bass drum of a marching band as I ran my hands over my body, checking for all my bits and pieces. I'd have bruises, but I was so relieved to be unhurt that I found myself laughing as I took my ponytail holder out and shook my hair. I'd never get all the sand out, not until I showered. I brushed the grit from my eyebrows and face and opened my eyes.

I was in a cave with a partially open ceiling. I got to my feet, legs quaking with adrenalin. Eventually my breathing slowed to normal and my heart calmed, but the hairs on the back of my neck suddenly rose into hackles. There was something, or someone, in this cave with me.

"He—hello?" My voice was soft in the deserted quiet. "Jesse? Is that you? Don't be playing jokes on me." My voice echoed eerily back to me.

No answer.

The cave was long and serpentine. Behind me, a long funnel of sand glimmered with starlight. I couldn't go back out that way; the rock on either side of the crevice I had fallen into was nearly vertical now that the sand had been swept away by my body.

Before me lay dark shadows and softly illuminated rock surfaces, curved and smooth and I knew it would be red in the daylight. The floor of the cave seemed to drop away downhill, and walls of rock jutted into the narrow canal, leaving my only path partially obstructed.

I began to walk, and shortly discovered why parts of the cave were illuminated. An open oculus overhead let in moon and starlight in shafts of soft light. Going slowly, my hackles still up, I went the only way I could go—down and through.

"Jesse?" I yelled louder this time and cocked my ear toward the hole as I passed under it. I half expected his face to block out the stars visible through the hole, and for him to yell down asking if I was all right. But I had lost Jesse even before I had slipped into this cave. He could even be in a cave of his own at the moment. "Jesse!" I called, and the name bounced off the walls, *esse... esse...*

The cave had to end, didn't it? As I rounded jutting corners protruding from the cave walls, my feet padding silently on the sand floor, I hoped to see an opening I could simply stroll out of. Another hole in the ceiling ahead lit my way like natural installations some creator knew would come in handy.

The sound of my breathing amplified in the small space and slowly, my hackles relaxed and the feeling of not being alone eased. Ahead of me, the cave widened into an cavern. Moonlight spilled in from the natural skylight, throwing the cavern into soft curves of shadow and light.

A gleam caught my eye as I entered the cavern. Something a little larger than my hand, and so black it seemed resinous and oily, was lodged in the rock across from me. As I strode toward it, I paused under the hole in the ceiling, looking up at the stars so high above me. I called for Jesse again, and listened. Still no answer.

Worry twisted in my gut. What if he had fallen, too? What if he'd broken an ankle or something? It was stupid, what we had done. It was something kids did. But it had been fun, until I'd come sliding down into this place. I turned my attention to finding a way out. Looking around, my heart plummeted. The cavern was closed in with no exit save for the way I'd come in.

I approached the black glinting thing and looked up at it, squinting. It was embedded just above eye level. It had to be obsidian. But what a strange place for it to be, wedged into the cave wall the way it was. It was the size of a coffee mug and so smooth I half expected it to run down the wall like oil. I reached up and laid a hand on the stone, expecting it to be cool and hard.

With a gasp, I jerked my hand back. The stone was *warm*. I touched it again. It was warmer than my hand and seemed to be pulsing softly—or was it my hand that was pulsing? Curiosity elbowed fear to the back of the line as my inner archaeologist woke up and rubbed her eyes. This was a *find*! Excitement at the idea of telling Ethan and Jesse and the rest of the team what I had found began to thrum in my torso. What was a polished piece of obsidian, *warm* obsidian, doing down here in some random cavern? The pulsing was probably just me, the oscillation of my heart responding to my strange predicament.

Was this cavern random? I looked around. The obsidian had to have been put here for a reason, embedded like an eye to watch this place for thousands of years. Another glint in the wall not quite opposite winked at me. There was a second stone embedded in the wall, at the same precise height as the first.

I gasped at the realization and crossed the cave in a hurry, heart pounding, mouth dry. What had I stumbled upon? This stone was also smooth, but in the dim light it appeared to be a light green color. Libyan desert glass. I had seen the stone in Ibukun's collection. I put a hand on the pale stone's smooth surface. It too, was warm, and there was that same pulse.

"Why are you here?" I asked the stone in wonder. "How did you get here?" More unspoken questions followed. Where am I? What is this place? Who put the stones into the wall?

And what the heck happened to Jesse?

"Jesse!" I went to stand under the hole in the ceiling, the stars winking down at me as though to say, *no trouble. There's no trouble here. There's been no trouble here ever, we've been watching.* "Jesse!" I called several times. I walked to the side of the cave I hadn't been to yet, peering up as the stars passed overhead, hoping for Jesse's voice or face to make a show.

My ankle rolled into a depression and I looked down. Two shallow holes were inset in the rock floor of the cavern. I bent down and brushed the sand out of the divots, realizing with a strange mixture of fear and wonder that the depressions were shaped sort of like *feet*. I felt around the edges. The stone had been sanded away, made smooth. Two long, gentle crescent shapes faced one another, together making a nearly perfect circle. These depressions were not accidental, either; they had to have been put here intentionally. I stood and stepped back, looking at them from higher up. A soft line of moonlight appeared as a shaft poured down into the cavern from the oculus at the top. The beam of light, soft though it was, highlighted motes in the air and streamed down like a gentle spotlight onto the crescents in front of me.

Hackles rose again on my neck, but this time they were not from fear. This was some kind of magic—the way the moonlight was traversing the floor, creeping its way across the crescents, slowly bringing them into the light. I watched, nearly breathless with wonder, as the moonbeam inched its way across the depressions.

Moved by some unexpected feeling from an unknown place, I kicked off my sneakers and left them on the rock behind me. The footprints were nearly fully illuminated now, beckoning.

I placed my bare feet in the crescents and gasped. The rock beneath me was also warm. My feet looked blue in the moonbeam and only the little toes of my left foot were still in shadow. The light traveled as I watched, transfixed. Inch by inch, it threw both my feet into light until the entire crescents along with my bare feet and legs were bathed in desert moonlight.

A wind swept through the cave, as sudden and fierce as a spring storm blowing in from across the Atlantic. But this was not an Atlantic wind; it was warm and dry. It picked up my hair, whirled it around, and slapped it into my face. I inhaled this new breeze but stiffened with shock because my lungs inflated and seemed not to stop. I tried to cry out at the feeling of my body taking in too much air. My lungs felt as though they were stretching to accommodate the wind, inflating like two zeppelins. My mind whirled and I tried again to scream. Tendrils of fear curled around my heart—what was happening to me?

I scanned the cave, my eyes darting about for an answer that was not forthcoming. The wind went on filling me. The obsidian and the desert glass and I made a perfect triangle, and I could imagine the vision saying, *you've finally noticed our little triumvirate, have you?* The stones lit and a pulse filled the cave. Not just the cave—the pulse filled me, and my heart matched its rhythm. It was an oscillation not of sound, but vibration. A hum like a giant generator filled my senses.

My feet lifted off the floor and my head and arms arched back. I felt stretched and far more buoyant than any human should be. The oscillation continued and my vision went white. My ears popped as the air pressure increased.

A scene unfolded in front of my blind eyes, painting my mind with color and life: an oasis of green, a backdrop of trees and flowers. Birds took to wing from the tops of palm trees and elephants grazed at the edge of a deep blue pool. A man appeared, materializing as though transitioning from smoke into flesh. Brown-skinned and wiry, with black wavy hair threaded with gray at his temples, he wore a simple black button-up shirt and dark denim pants. His hands were graceful and beautiful, the tapered fingers long and elegant—a musician's hands. The angles of his face were familiar but I had never seen him before, I was sure of it. It was his eyes that held my attention; they were gray too, as light as a dove's breast, just like mine. As I watched, they took on a silver cast which swirled like mercury laced with streams of white paint. He had my chin, my lips, the shape of my brow. Or did I have his?

Dad?

I had only thought the word, but it filled the air with the sound of a million voices on the wind all speaking in unison.

The man's face changed. It softened as if in response and his chin tilted down in a partial nod. But his movements were extremely slow, like he was trapped in a dream which forced him to move at a mere quarter of his normal speed.

I thought my heart would explode but it held steady, matching the pulse filling my head and all around me.

The question hung in the air, and a second flock of birds, cranes, exploded from the bush and took to the darkening sky.

His face moved in slow motion, he blinked his eyes slowly closed, then opened them again. His lips parted and tightened to form a word. His brows drew together and one arm moved slowly up from his side, his hand reaching toward me. Those silver eyes filled with urgency. Silently, and very slowly, he said one simple word. It was unmistakeable, even for someone unaccustomed to lipreading.

Run.

My skin prickled. That strange oscillation of which I was part continued playing without ceasing. A fork of bright lightning stabbed down from the sky and thunder whacked as the scene went black.

I collapsed on the cave floor, trembling and out of breath. My sight returned and I covered my eyes and rolled them under my fingertips. I coughed and choked, struggling for my lungs to return to normal.

As I lay there gasping, a second vision came, though not nearly as real and vivid as the first. It was of a newborn, sweet and vulnerable in her mother's arms. She was working for that first inhale of life. I gasped and sucked in an enormous breath and winced as my lungs came unstuck as though they had never breathed before. Whispered words found my ears: *The first breath is where it all begins.*

My heart flew to my chest where my system felt stretched and aching. As my breathing calmed, I looked up at the black stone, then to the green one. They sat there dormant, as though nothing had happened. They remained unchanged. Unlike me.

"What was that?" I asked the stone. My own voice frightened me. I took stock of my body as I slowly got to my feet. My chest and heart calmed and the aching had ceased, and yet, why did my torso feel like a barrel of dormant energy? My heart no longer felt like a flexing muscle, pushing blood through my system. I closed my eyes. No, instead it felt like a throbbing battery of energy. The difference was unmistakeable. Like an energy cell of some kind, sending out small repeated booms of power as it beat.

I slowed my breathing to concentrate on this difference, and became like a sleeping person–an observer in their own dream, watching things like a god who could reach out and change things if she so chose. Reaching out a curious mental finger at this energy cell living in my chest, I asked the pulse to speed up. It responded obediently. I asked it to slow down. It responded again. I asked it to cease. It did not cease, it held steady as if to say: *Ask me anything and I will give it to you, but if my rhythm ceases, you die. I am your heart.*

I opened my eyes and looked down at my hands. They were still my flesh and blood but had somehow become more than that. They too, were conductors and receivers of energy, each finger a tendril of power. What could be done with these limbs now? I didn't know. And that frightened me.

I looked down at my feet and at the floor, and something else frightened me.

The crescent-shaped depressions in the cave floor were gone.

I squatted, suddenly panting and startled, the battery of my heart jumping. I ran my hands over the floor. The light in here was dim as the moon had moved her glow elsewhere. Perhaps I just couldn't see them in the shadows? But the floor was smooth and cool to the touch. The footprints were no longer there; my eyes had not deceived me.

I looked up at the desert glass, now dull in the quiet nighttime gloom. I crossed the cave and reached up to touch it. It was cool and silent. Wait. Not silent. I closed my eyes and felt that it had a pulse all its own. I let out a laugh of wonder and opened my eyes.

Keeping my palm against the glass, I tuned in to my heart. My heart had its pulse and the glass had its pulse, and the two oscillated in their own rhythms, not meeting but skipping around one another, every third beat matching. I slowed my heart to meet the pulse of the glass. Like a runner joining another on the road, I fell into step with the crystal.

SHHH-CRACK!

I screamed reflexively, my heart jumping back to its own rhythm, as the glass shattered and exploded across the cave. Shards of glass sprayed the floor, tinkling with a thousand dry *tik tik tiks*. Silence descended again.

Breathing hard, I stared at the mess I'd made. Something like terror crept up behind me and traced its fingers up my back. I realized two things at once: though I was standing directly in front of the glass, not a shard had touched me. My face and chest should have been embedded with hundreds of tiny scimitars, but I was unscathed.

The second realization was that I had destroyed something beautiful, something meaningful and mysterious, and I hadn't meant to.

My hand flew to cover my mouth. I was horrified at what I had done. The light glinted dully off the shattered glass coating the cave floor. Where the glass had been, there was now nothing but a depression in the stone. An empty shadow. Regret soured in my mouth. *What have you done?*

"Petra?"

I gave a startled scream and looked up. "Jesse?"

"Petra, I was going crazy. What happened to you? Are you okay?"

Good question.

The light in the cave dimmed as a shadow moved across the oculus. "How did you get down there? My God, Petra." Jesse's voice filled with concern. "Did you fall?"

"Sort of." I peered through the oculus. I was afraid to move my feet as the floor was covered in glass and I hadn't put my shoes back

on yet. Jesse's head was nothing but a black silhouette. "I hit some
loose sand and I slid. There's an opening on the other side. Jesse, I—"
but words did not come. Where did I even begin? "I can't get out
without help."

He snorted. "No kidding. I've been looking for you for half an
hour. Why didn't you yell for me?"

"I did. Maybe not enough. I'm sorry."

"Don't be sorry, for Pete's sake. I'm just relieved that you're okay.
Can you wait a little longer while I go get a rope?"

"Of course."

"Hang tight, I'll be right back." His head disappeared.

"Jesse!"

The shadow reappeared. "Yeah?"

"Don't run," I said. "And don't step where it looks like sand has
coated the rock. There might be no rock under it. That's how I fell in
here."

"Sure. Okay." He paused, but I couldn't see his expression.
"You're sure you're all right? Nothing broken or sprained?"

"I'm fine." It wasn't exactly a lie. I *am* fine, I thought. I'm just
different.

As I waited for Jesse, I put my hand against the cave wall and
closed my eyes. It, too, had a pulse. I could feel it thrumming quietly
under my hand. I took my hand away. I did not dare match its rhythm
with my heart. I crossed the cave and put my hand on the obsidian.
The pulse was there, too, different yet again to the glass and the cave.
Its rhythm was closer to my own heart's rhythm than anything else I
had touched before it. I snatched my hand away in fear. The last
thing I wanted to do was destroy it accidentally.

I realized that based on what had just happened, I had the means
to get myself out of here without any help. I had the means to shatter
the cave into dust and walk from the rubble untouched.

I bent and put my hands near the floor, turning my palms toward
the far wall. With an easy mental shove, the shards of glass blew
across the rock and piled up along the wall. I padded across the cave

to my shoes and pulled them on, then I stood under the hole in the ceiling and waited.

———

"YOU SURE YOU'RE OKAY?" asked Jesse, after he'd lifted me from the cave and up through the hole in the ceiling. His hands squeezed my shoulders, my biceps, my elbows, my ribcage, then pulled me in for a hug.

"I'm okay." I breathed in his scent and hugged him back. "Just a little frightened."

"Yeah, no doubt!" He released me from the hug and put his palms on either side of my face. He peered into my eyes. His expression was partially shrouded in shadow but I could make out the concern there. "You seem so calm. It's freaking me out a little."

I gave a shaky laugh. "You want me to cry?"

He hugged me again. "No, of course not. I'm just not sure I would have handled that as well as you are."

"I knew you would come along," I said. But it was filler. I hadn't been thinking about Jesse at all while I was hanging suspended above the cave floor, my lungs feeling like they might pop, and a vision of someone who looked like he could be my father invading my mind. My smile faltered at the thought of the man with the silver eyes. I could still see the lines of his face as they grew serious, his lips as they formed a directive I did not understand.

Run.

Run from what? Run from who? There was no one dangerous here. I was surrounded by a bunch of archaeologists and researchers, history geeks just like me. We had sponsorship dollars, we had security. I felt completely safe. I thought of the man at the airport and the strange symbol on his wrist. But he was long gone and far away. Surely not a threat.

Jesse helped me get to me feet and we made our way toward the camp. He threaded his fingers through mine and didn't let go of my hand the entire way back. I could feel the pulse of his heart distinctly through his fingers. My fingers grew cold at the horrifying thought of Jesse exploding if I matched my heartbeat to his and I almost dropped his hand. I shoved the unwelcome thought away almost violently. Jesse stopped when we were still outside of earshot of the cluster of tents and vehicles.

"Maybe, we—" he began, his voice in a whisper.

"Should keep this between us?"

He let out a breath. "Yeah."

"Fine by me." The fewer questions I got about what had happened to me in that cave, the better.

I moved to start walking again and Jesse stopped me and pulled me around to face him. We stood there face to face, breathing together in the dark.

"You really scared me, Petra. I'm not sure I've ever been that scared." Then he added with a head bob, "My baby sister got bit by a spider once and started throwing up, that was pretty scary. But since then—" He cupped my face with a palm and tucked my hair behind my ear with his fingers. His hands were cool and a little clammy. Fear does that.

My pulse sped up a fraction. The last time someone had shown this kind of concern about my well-being was when I had wandered away from my group on a school trip and become lost. It was the unadulterated relief that slumped Beverly's shoulders when the police delivered me to her front door. Deliverance from her worst nightmare made her clutch me for so long I thought we'd get stuck in that hug, her muscles quivering and her tears wetting my hair and clothes. The experience had hammered into my preteen brain—I was loved, and not knowing my whereabouts had caused Beverly a horrible pain. This wasn't entirely the same, but the authenticity of Jesse's concern filled my body with warmth. I did not doubt his care for me in that moment, and that was a rare thing.

He pulled my forehead to his and I wrapped my hands around his wrists.

"Petra," he said. "I just have the weirdest feeling that something happened to you in that cave." His words were stilted, unsure.

"What makes you say that?" My heart jumped another notch.

"I don't know." He held me there, not releasing me from his grip. His dark eyes looked into mine. "Am I wrong?"

"I'm okay, Jesse."

"That's not—" He finally let my forehead go, but pulled back to get a better look at me. Moonlight brushed the bones of his face, his cheekbones, his forehead, his strong straight nose, his lips. "I'm glad you're okay, but *something* did happen to you. Didn't it."

A beat.

"Maybe," I finally admitted.

He almost seemed relieved and let out a pent-up breath. When I said no more, he added, "You can talk to me. Anytime. You know that, right?"

I nodded. My own hands were cool and clammy by this time and my thoughts were racing. How had Jesse picked up that something had happened to me? And how would I even describe what had happened?

I had to show the cave to the team, it was too important a find not to. But then, how would I explain the shards of desert glass lining the wall?

Overwhelm sat its heavy body on both my shoulders and its brother, fatigue, joined the party. "Let's go." I made for camp. "I'm tired, and I'm sure you are too."

"All right, Petra." His disappointment was palpable.

We finished the journey to the site and after a final hug, Jesse crawled into his tent and I crawled into mine.

ELEVEN

I had just finished dumping my bucket of excavated dirt into a tray to begin the dry-screening process when the wind kicked up, blew my hat off, picked up some of the dirt and threw it into my face and eyes. I blinked and lifted my hand to brush the dirt and sand from eyes when I heard Jesse's voice behind me.

"Your hands are dirty, that'll make it worse. Let me. I've been wearing gloves." Warm hands took my face. "Can you look up?"

I tried to look up but had to blink rapidly. Thumbs gently pulled down the grit from the corner of my right eye.

"That better?"

"The left one is worse, actually," I said, trying to hold still.

Another powerful gust of wind blew over us, throwing sand and dirt into the air like confetti and whipping our clothes against our limbs. It was followed by a second more powerful blast that made Jesse and me bend our faces into each other's shoulders. Annoyed voices cried out from the excavation pit.

"Throw your tarps over and take shelter!" Ethan's voice called over the wind.

Jesse and I tucked our buckets away into the shelving under the tables and worked to cover our trench with the emergency tarps we had for just this reason. Winds could kick up out of nowhere and we couldn't have them tearing apart our pits. We finished and Jesse took my hand.

"Come on." Jesse led me, head bent against the wind and eyes mostly closed as more dust and sand whipped us in the face, stinging our cheeks.

"My tent is the closest." I stumbled after him, the wind tearing the words from my mouth. But he heard me and I felt him redirect.

We fumbled our way, half-blind, through my tent door, both of us squatting in close proximity as Jesse zipped the door shut. The calm inside the tent made me breathe a sigh of relief.

Keeping my eyes closed, I took off my long sleeved white button-up and shook it. I took my hair out of its low ponytail and ran my fingers through it. I felt the movement of Jesse brushing sand away, too.

"Ugh." I felt the grit that had built up on my scalp and on the back of my neck. "Sand everywhere, and I still can barely see." My eyes were stinging.

"Here." Jesse fingers found my face again. He removed the sand from my eyes as best he could, until I could finally open them. We were crouched together in the entrance compartment of my tent, and when he finally came into focus, my heart tripped. His face was startlingly close to mine.

I unzipped the inner door and reached in to grab my toiletries bag. Retrieving a bottle of spray and a towel, I gave my hands as good a wash as I could before crawling through and into my tent. I kicked off my runners and left them in the first compartment.

"We're going to get sand in your house." Jesse had to raise his voice over the sound of the wind outside.

"I've had sand in my bed from day one. The stuff gets absolutely everywhere."

"Ain't that the truth," he agreed, crawling in behind me and zipping the tent door closed.

We sprawled onto my bed and lay on our backs looking up at the tent ceiling. The wind howled and the barrage of sand against the canvas was loud and unrelenting.

"Sounds almost like we've angered some god," I said.

"Yeah. I think that's what the locals think too. This is the promise of much worse winds to come," said Jesse, eyes staring upward and head slightly cocked to the side. He'd taken off his shirt to use as a headrest and lay there in a white tank top. In the dim light, his skin looked even darker than normal against the contrast of the light fabric. I noticed a cord around his neck, the end of it disappeared under his shirt. I thought of asking him what the necklace carried when he said, "This is the Ghibli."

"There's a name for this storm?"

Jesse nodded. "It's seasonal, and it's caused enough damage over the centuries to warrant a title." He turned onto his side to face me, tucking his folded shirt under his cheekbone. "Every summer, a hot dry wind blows up from the Sahara toward the Mediterranean. It can reach hurricane speed by the time it hits the coast of North Africa." He paused as the wind and sand gave a particularly violent bash against the walls of my tent.

"Geez, I hope we don't fly away. Maybe we should have run for one of the vehicles," I murmured.

"Frightened?" Jesse examined my face.

I shook my head. "You?"

"I'm okay. It won't get that bad. This is just the start of the season. We'll be gone before the real Ghibli hits. Thankfully."

"Why would they plan this dig for when they knew the winds picked up?" I put up a hand. "Not that I'm complaining. I would have come even if we had to use ice-picks to excavate the site from under a glacier."

"Ethan has a contract with the sponsors. The site has to be excavated by a certain date. We're the last team to be scheduled before the dig pauses for the summer."

I gasped as the walls of the tent whipped tautly in and out, snapping loudly. Jesse put a hand on my wrist and his thumb stroked across my pulse. I swallowed and my heart rate increased a notch. A warm feeling flushed through my stomach.

"How long do you think this will last?"

"Hard to say," Jesse said, as we stared at each other in the strange dun-colored light. "Worst case scenario is that we'll be stuck in here for the night." A dimple appeared in his cheek. "All alone. Just the two of us." His eyes dropped to my lips.

I cleared my throat and lowered my voice to a whisper, "With the Ghibli screaming her fury around us and throwing sand all over our work."

Jesse closed his eyes and rolled his face into his shirt. He groaned dramatically. "Ugh. It's going to be a disaster out there when this is over." He let go of my wrist and rolled onto his back. He rubbed both hands over his eyes. "Ethan is going to be furious. Even if the tarps stay down, this will put us behind."

"He knew it could happen," I said. "We talked about it at orientation."

"Yeah." He turned his head to look at me again. "But there's always hope right, that things will go as smoothly as possible."

I nodded and turned on my side to face him. We gazed at each other and listened to the storm for several minutes.

Jesse surprised me by putting a hand to my cheek. "Are you okay?"

"I'm fine," I said with surprise. "I mean, I'm glad I'm not weathering this storm alone, but I'm totally fine. Why?"

"I don't mean about the storm."

"You mean about falling into the cave? Why wouldn't I be?" I kept my features calm but inside, my heart had begun to hammer. Why was Jesse so insistent that something major had happened to me that night? He wasn't wrong; it was just weird that he was so intuitive about it.

Jesse's shoulder lifted in an elegant shrug. "You've been pretty quiet since then. At meals. While you're working." He took his hand from my cheek. "I'm not the only one who's noticed. Some of us are worried about you."

"Who else is worried about me?"

"Ibby. Ethan. Those of us who've gotten to know you a bit better."

I frowned. Was it really that obvious? "There is nothing to worry about. I'm just focused on the work. You know this is my dream job, right? It'll be over before we realize it. I want to make it count."

"Mm-hmm," Jesse said, like he didn't quite believe me. "If that's true, you really are an overachiever."

I laughed. "You sound like my therapist."

A gust of wind threw more sand over our tent than I even wanted to think about.

Unexpectedly, Jesse scooted closer to me and pressed his lips against my cheek. His warm stubble scratched pleasantly across my skin and my heart exploded like a thoroughbred from the starting gate. The sudden coming alive of my body was as much a shock to me as the kiss was. If Jesse had meant the kiss to be sweet and platonic, he had radically failed. Jesse pulled back, but kept his face close. In his eyes reflected the same surprise at the electricity between us and I heard him take a quick breath. My cheek tingled where all the blood had rushed to the surface. We surged toward each other, moving like a set of magnets compelled to make contact.

Jesse met my lips with his and suddenly his weight was half on top of me and we were straining against each other, our arms wrapping around one another as though we couldn't get close enough. My heart felt as though it was throwing itself against my ribcage, my fingers wound through his hair, oblivious to the sand that fell onto my face and trickled across my skin.

The Ghibli screamed around the tent, the sharp sound of sand against the canvas drowning out the sound of our kiss. I felt a rumble in Jesse's chest as he pulled me on top of him, his hand rucking up the bottom of my tank top of find the skin of my ribs.

Jesse's heartbeat became audible to me, pulsing not just in my ears but against my body. Underneath his heartbeat, a second rhythm was detectable; a faster oscillation which grew stronger as his lips moved against mine and the thrumming of our bodies ramped up. The strange pulse seemed to reach toward me and then wrap around me like a cocoon enfolding both of us. It called forth my own rhythm and the two began to play a little rhythmic game. I couldn't tell whose was faster but I could tell that the rhythms were working to get in sync with one another. What would happen when the frequencies met?

The memory of the rupturing desert glass exploded into my memory and shattered my pleasure with panic. I gasped and pulled back, my heart pounding and chest heaving. I sat up, my thighs on either side of Jesse's hips. His eyes opened wide with surprise, hands reaching for me.

"What's wrong?" Then a look of horror crossed his face. "I'm sorry. Are you okay?" He sat up underneath me and put his palms on my waist. "I thought you liked it—"

"I did!" I said, hating the look of panic I'd put on his face. "Don't apologize, I loved it, really." I put a hand to where my heart was hammering under my breastbone and ribs. The sensation of our two rhythms was gone and I let out a long sigh of relief. My hands were trembling. There was no way of explaining this to him.

I wove my fingers through his hair and kissed his lips and his cheeks and across his jaw, wanting nothing more than to erase the distress from his features and then keep kissing him and never stop. But fear had rattled me. I had destroyed that desert glass by matching its rhythm to my own. What would happen to Jesse if I let our frequencies meet in the same way?

"It's just a little fast," I said, finally, to give him some kind of explanation.

He let out a pent-up breath and I felt him nod against me. "Okay," he whispered, wrapping his arms around me and giving me a hug. He kissed my ear, my neck. "You're in charge, Petra," he said, his lips moving against my ear and sending shivers of pleasure down my spine. "Whatever you want. Whatever makes you happy."

His words made me melt, made me want to tear his clothes off, and made me want to scream with frustration at the unexplained powers I suddenly had. *Was* I dangerous to him? Was there a way I could find out?

"Thank you." I held him close as the wind and sand cycloned around the tent.

He pulled back and smiled at me, brushing my sandy hair away from my face. We listened as the wind bellowed, gazing at one another in the near-darkness.

"I wonder what the others are up to?" I listened for any sign of life outside the tent.

Jesse pressed another kiss to my mouth and grinned, his teeth gleaming in the dark. "Not this, I can assure you."

I laughed as he rolled me over onto the bed, pressing his stomach against my back, spooning me. Between the two of us, there was too much heat, but neither of us seemed to care so we lay there spooning and waiting out the storm.

TWELVE

The vision of the man with the silver-gray eyes haunted me every night that week. I saw him in my dreams and behind my eyelids whenever I closed my eyes. I never saw him as clearly as I'd seen him in the cave, but the intensity of his message remained the same. I became edgy and mildly paranoid, watching the security team when they didn't know I was looking. My ears perked at conversations had within hearing distance. I saw nothing, heard nothing that hinted of danger. After a week of this, I told myself I was being silly. I might never get to be on a dig in Libya again. How could I enjoy the experience if I was constantly jumping at shadows?

I felt Jesse's eyes on me frequently as the dig progressed. I would catch him looking and he would look away, but not before I caught the look of concern, and if I wasn't mistaken, sadness. It reminded me of the sadness I'd felt on his thoughts during the team orientation meeting back in Saltford. Concern I could understand, but sadness? I reassured him in whispered words twice over meals in the mess tent that I was fine. He would nod and smile and squeeze my arm, but the concern and sadness did not go away.

Then I caught Ibby doing the same thing, her eyes lingering on me, charged with worry. She'd look away quickly as soon as my eyes met hers. I began to wonder if Jesse had said something to her. I asked him at the dry-screening table as we sifted through our sand and dirt for finds. He assured me he hadn't said anything to anyone about that night, and I believed him.

As one week slipped into the next, the events in the cave haunted me less frequently. I still hadn't made up my mind to tell Ethan about the cave. I was dying to share the discovery with the team, but I still wasn't sure how to explain the presence of the glass–unless I didn't say anything about it at all. But leaving out such an important feature grated unbearably against my professional sensitivities. The glass had been embedded in the wall by someone, for some reason. I couldn't believe that the stones had been put there just to wait for me to come along. And so I wrestled with myself until the day came when I had a much bigger problem than the discovery of the cave.

I was treading across the sand to the mess tent to refill my water bottle when a movement at the nearest basalt monolith caught my eye. The rock had swayed, I was certain of it. I stopped walking and narrowed my eyes, thinking I had perhaps experienced some trick of vision. Ibby and Jesse were working in the trench in the shadow of the crooked monolith, seemingly deep in discussion. The stone shifted again and I gasped. The top of the monolith had moved, probably mere centimeters but I had *seen* it move.

"Ibby! Jesse!" I dropped my bottle, which went rolling away across the sand. "Get out of the trench!" My heart leapt in my chest as the top of the huge stone shifted again. It had been a microscopic movement but this time, I felt the vibration under my feet, just for a moment before it stopped again. I broke into a run. "Move!" I screamed.

Jesse and Ibby and every other person in the camp watched me in surprise as I bolted across the sand toward my friends.

"Petra, what the—" Ibby's voice and expression was full of confusion, but had she known the danger she was in, it would have been full of terror. Her lack of understanding turned my blood to ice. Jesse was getting to his feet, but Ibby was still on her knees. I felt a sound of frustration tear at my throat. Why did she not understand?

The monolith moved again, and this time it did not stop moving. It telegraphed full intent to topple over and crush my teammates. There was a groan of grinding rock from its base. Ibby and Jesse looked up and understood what was happening. It was unmistakeable now, to anyone who had a set of working eyes. Both of their faces paled with shock and fear.

They scrambled to their feet, but their movements seemed so slow and laborious. Why weren't they moving faster? They'd never be free of the falling stone in time.

I could hear the grinding crush of stone against stone and dense compacted sand being disturbed as the basalt pedestal that had held the stone upright for a millennium finally gave way. The years of wind and shifting sands had finally worn it down. It was a moment that was mathematically certain to happen. But incredulity that the moment had arrived when my friends were in its shadow flushed my limbs with shock and adrenalin. I had to *do* something. This could not happen!

Its top, so far away and cast in sharp relief against the blue of the sky, drifted across my vision and flooded my stomach with a sickening vertigo. My inertia broke like a wave.

I vaulted the string cordoning off the trench and baseball-slid on my hip between Jesse and Ibby as they scrambled to get out of the way.

I heard someone scream my name but I couldn't tell which of my friends it was.

Jesse's fingers grazed my arm as I flew by. A deep sonorous frequency emitted itself from my chest and began to repeat on an endless loop. I felt my heart hum like a generator. I slid onto my back in the shadow of the falling stone and held my palms face up. A cold certainty that what I was doing would work replaced my terror.

There were screams in the back of my mind but I didn't know if they were real or imagined. I ignored them. The pounding resonance continued, my cells quaked with it; my heart *was* the drum making this beat. The creak became a scream as the stone fell faster and the monolith made to crush me. It tilted dramatically, making to crash on the earth. Then it froze, as I knew it would, mere inches from my hands. The base of the single monstrous rock swung upward as it leveled out. Rubble and stones broke away and fell. I became the fulcrum on which the slab rested and balanced.

Jesse and Ibby should have been at least partially crushed, and me completely, but I held the stone there as my friends scrambled free. The monolith hovered, still and waiting, as the power emanating from my body supported it. Mentally, I pushed the monolith away and it reversed its course, slowly tipping upright once again.

But halfway through the procedure of righting the stone, I recognized a problem. My sonic booms were being diluted as the monolith slowly erected, their energy diffusing around the rock and up into the sky. I paused the stone there, thinking, ruminating about what to do with the massive rock now hovering overtop of me.

I could try punching the rock upward with a single powerful blast and scramble out of the way before letting it fall again, but it might not be enough. Instead of taking that risk, I chose to keep the stone where it was, allowing it to level off perpendicular to the earth again. When the stone was still, I gave it a mental push to slide it to the left. I rolled to the right and let my sonic booms die. The hum in my body went silent as the stone dropped with a crack, landing mere inches from my body. Sand blew over me and I squeezed my eyes shut and turned my face away.

Near silence descended. My own breathing was all I could hear.

I couldn't regret what I had done. Jesse and Ibby would have been seriously injured or killed, that I knew for certain. But there was no doubt in my mind that every single team member had just witnessed what had happened. So much for my secret. I got to my feet, keeping my eyes down. I wasn't ready yet to see the looks on their faces.

I brushed the sand from my hair, face, and clothes and looked at the monster stone lying across the dig pit. I took several breaths before I had enough courage to look up. No one had said anything or moved a muscle, as far as I could tell.

Jesse and Ibby stood the nearest. Ibby was down on her knees, and Jesse was on his back. Both of them seemed like mannequins from a haunted-house, their faces pale and eyes stretched so wide I could see the whites of them. Beyond Jesse and Ibby was Ethan, his hat dangling from one hand while his other hand shielded his eyes. He too was frozen; only his hair and hat moved in the desert wind.

The security team and our dig-labor from Ghat stood scattered about like toy soldiers. Here, a disembodied head frozen and staring from across the top of a Jeep. There, a figure with his hands held on either side of his head stuck in a parody of surprise. The shocked faces of our dig-crew peered in my direction from several pits. Figures were poised outside the mess tent, one with a broken cup at his feet and a wet patch in the sand, another with a hand on the arm of a companion. Every face stared, every body was still, every eye was locked on me.

It seemed as though the camp was stuck there for an eternity. No one knew what to do, what to say. Until—

"Euroklydon," came a fearful whisper on the wind.

My head cocked at the sound, searching for its source.

"Euroklydon." This time it came from somewhere else, and now louder.

"Euroklydon, Euroklydon!" This time it was a bellow of fear and it was joined by many others like it was a cry of 'fire!' Every cry had come from the members of the security team or our dig labor. I stood there frozen in surprise, as did every one of the dig team members. The security team and laborers began to run. At first they seemed frantic and directionless, but then began to head toward the vehicles. They snatched up hats, weapons, backpacks, things were hurriedly tossed into the back of two Jeeps. The cries of 'Euroklydon' lessened, but it was a word that hung in the air, laced with fear.

"Wait!" It was Ethan, putting up a hand and looking around at the chaos, aghast. "What's happening?"

"Euroklydon!" was the only answered cry, spoken as if it should be reason enough to vacate the premise immediately.

Jeeps roared to life and drivers jammed the accelerators, pulling the vehicles through the camp and in wide circles, kicking up sand and knocking over three tents. A large tub full of precious water was knocked over and went gushing across the desert floor, sucked up by the greedy sand in mere moments.

"Wait! Please, wait!" Ethan ran after the Jeeps, floundering in the sand and falling to a knee.

"Wait! Where are you going?" Jesse had joined in the call and put a hand out alongside the closest Jeep as it screamed by him. He ran for a time, following the tire treads, his hand up and his voice calling, begging for them to stop.

My jaw hung open in shock.

We watched our entire security team and our local labor disappear over a dune in the horizon. They'd left only the van and one other Jeep. A couple of face masks caught in a gust of wind blew across the desert sand, rolling like small tumbleweeds.

The vehicles reappeared as specks on a dune in the beyond, only to disappear again for good. Jesse stood there watching the horizon for a time, his fingers laced over the top of his head, elbows jutting out and shoulders lifting and dropping with his breath. He turned and followed the tire tracks back to us, his dark eyes flashing to me momentarily, the dark slashes of his brows drawn together. He bent and helped Ethan get to his feet.

"What just happened?" Ibby cried, her hands flying to her cheeks. "I don't understand what's happening."

Finally, my legs moved and I joined Ibby as we approached Jesse and Ethan. Sarah and Chris emerged from their trench, pale and shocked. Chris had an arm around Sarah's shoulders. Everyone seemed out of breath, though only Jesse and Ethan had been running.

Jesse's eyes were wild with shock, his brown hand clutched his heart and his face mask dangled around his neck. Ethan had a hand over his heart also, breathing deeply, but he looked much less panicked than Jesse. I stared at his face, trying to work out his expression. It seemed he might understand something the rest of us didn't.

Ethan's eyes met mine. "Euroklydon," he wheezed.

"What's that?" Ibby asked, almost screaming in her distress. She took a breath. "Sorry to yell. But what the hell just happened? Why did they all run away?" She spread her arms wide and slapped them down on her thighs with a thwack that proclaimed she was at her wits' end. "What on earth is a Euroklydon?"

"It's not a what." Ethan clapped his hat on his head where it sat off-kilter. With his eyes locked on mine, he said, "It's a who."

THIRTEEN

Ibby handed me a glass of water and I took it, numbly, and drank. Jesse had started a fire in the pit and we had made our way there like a group of staggering zombies and sat down. Ibby poured and handed water to the rest of the group. Looks darted my way like eyeballs were on a timer. Couldn't blame them.

I sipped the water and sat on a stone with my hoody draped over my shoulders. For the first time since we'd arrived at the dig site, the evening air was cool enough to warrant a layer, but just barely. We watched the flames dance in the desert wind as the sky suggested that it was thinking about dusk.

"Who is Euroklydon?" I asked Ethan as he set his camp chair in the sand and sat down.

"I'm not sure I can explain very well." Ethan removed his hat and brushed a hand over his thinning silver hair. "There isn't much to read on it, but the word appears in ancient texts, including the Bible. In scripture, it's a tempest from the east, a wind of biblical proportions which swept up and destroyed Paul's ship. But it is mentioned in other texts a time or two, more as a kind of deity, a controller of winds." Ethan shrugged. "That's all I know. I'll be looking into it more deeply, I can tell you that." He paused, meditating, then held up a finger. "Our labor was all from Ghat."

"And?" Jesse prompted.

"But only three of our security team were Libyan, there was one Egyptian, and one from Algeria originally. I only know that because Jody told me. Yet, they all knew the name Euroklydon. Seems somewhat universal to North Africa, at least." He brought the finger to the end of his nose, as he sometimes did when pontificating. "And they all fear it."

Ibby leaned forward, her sharp pixie's face homing in on me like a compass needle. She propped her elbows on her knees. "How did you do it, Petra?" She paused before adding, "*Why* you did, that part is clear. And thank you for that. But how?"

"I don't know," I answered quietly, looking down at my feet and digging at the sand with the toes of my sneakers. I didn't regret what I did, but it had been so *public*, and so...un-hideable. I couldn't even pretend that it had been anything other than what it was–catching and lifting a massive stone, with what appeared to be just a force emitting from my body.

"You don't know? How can you not know? You looked like you knew exactly what you were doing. It was written all over you." Her body became more animated, her expression more open. "Don't get me wrong, it was awesome. You are badass, and I am totally intimidated by you right now. But what the—"

"Have you ever done anything like that before?" Ethan interrupted, shooting a look at Ibby that said: *back off a little.*

I opted for the truth. "Not on that scale."

"But you have lifted something like that before?" Ibby jumped into the opening my words had left. "With your mind?"

I nodded, keeping my eyes on the sand. "I have always had a low-grade telekinesis. For as long as I can remember."

Ethan seemed oddly satisfied by this admission, and tilted his chair back in the sand. The front legs came off the ground a few inches.

"*Low-grade?*" Ibby barked out a laugh and shook her head. "Unbelievable."

"Petra." Jesse spoke for the first time since our team had deserted us. I looked up at him and his green eyes were limpid pools that drowned me in compassion. "Something *did* happen to you..."

He didn't have to finish the sentence. I knew what he meant.

In that cave.

"It makes no sense that you know that," I said. "You weren't there. But you're right."

Jesse sat back, satisfied. He opened his hands wide as if to say *so, explain.*

"Where? What?" Ibby looked from Jesse to me and back again. "I'm confused again. I can't keep up here, people."

My eyes on Jesse, I addressed the group. "I fell into a strange cave a little over a week ago."

"You did what?" Ethan's eyes popped and the front legs of his camping chair thudded down into the sand. "How? When?"

"It was that still night we had. I couldn't sleep, so I got up. Jesse was awake, too. We ran along the tops of those rocks." I gestured to the reddish hulks of stone beyond the campsite.

"At night?" Ethan goggled. "You could have broken your leg!" He pawed his forehead with frustration. "God save me from kids who think they're immortal."

"I could have. But I didn't. I slid into a cave and Jesse pulled me out."

Jesse's eyes stayed on my face, waiting, knowing there was more.

"Am I the only one who isn't getting it?" Ibby asked after too much silence had passed.

"What happened in the cave?" Jesse prompted.

My lips parted, but words seemed inadequate.

"Would it help if we took them there?" Jesse straightened and put his hands on the armrests of his camp chair.

"I don't know if I could find it again." But this wasn't true. The cave was archaeologically significant. I made certain to remember the path we took on the way back to our tents that night.

"I can," said Jesse. "I made the journey to that cave three times that night."

"Why three?" Ethan asked.

"I had to get rope to help Petra out."

Ibby stood up. "Well, what are we waiting for? If this cave has something to do with how you lifted that rock today, we need to see it. How far is it?"

"Maybe half an hour's walk. We still have a couple of hours of light." Jesse eyed the horizon. "We'll be slow if we walk on the sand, though."

"Then we'll walk on the stones." Ethan got to his feet. "Slowly, and in the light of day."

I looked up at Ethan with surprise. I hadn't expected him to go along with the idea so quickly. He was responsible for us and a stickler for safety. But there he was, lacing up his shoes. They were all ready, looking at me. I pulled my hoody on and stood, doing up the zipper. I looked at Jesse. "Lead the way."

Jesse retraced our steps just the way I would have, skirting the sandier tops of stone and using the wider rocks as our path. We walked in silence, eyes down, taking it slow. My mind whirled as we made the journey and I walked at the rear, brooding. I wasn't worried that they wouldn't believe me, for the shattered glass and what they saw happen today was plenty of evidence that my story was not an invention. It was the *now what?* that had sent my brain into paroxysms of potential scenarios. No one had ever known my secret until I had told it to Noel, my therapist, and now many other people knew, and most of them had gone running for the hills screaming a word I'd never heard before.

Euroklydon.

"This must be where you fell in." Jesse's voice snapped me out of my mental musings. Our group stopped where sand coated the top of the rock and broken edges told of a cave-in.

I nodded.

Ethan looked into the dark hole and then up at me, horrified. "It's a miracle you didn't get hurt!"

"I think the miracle was lifting a forty ton block of stone with her mind," injected Ibby. "Not to be disagreeable, but is there an easier way inside? I'm not keen on going down this hole. Looks like a place scorpions would live." She shivered.

"Just ahead," said Jesse. "There's a bigger hole right overtop the cave where I found her."

We walked further until the oculus over the cave came into view. Jesse rigged up a rope ladder by fastening it securely to a nearby spike of stone. He gestured that I should go first, so I lowered myself back into the strange place. My breath echoed back at me and the sound of my shoes on the cave floor told of layers of grit which had blown inside and coated the rock since my last visit.

The cave seemed commonplace in the evening light. I moved away from the rope ladder to give Ibby room and scanned the walls. The obsidian stone glittered from its place in the wall and the line of shattered desert glass lay pushed up against the side where I had left it.

My heart sped up when I saw something that I hadn't noticed before. Lines scratched into the cave walls had been invisible in the gloom of night, but the waning daylight caught the shallow grooves and made them stand out.

"My heavens," breathed Ethan as he touched the ground and moved aside, almost tripping over his own feet as he stared at our surroundings. "This is remarkable! Is that obsidian?"

Ibby was kneeling near the wall and leaned her face down to the pile of shattered glass on the floor. She gingerly picked up a larger piece and peered at it. "Desert tektite." She looked up at the stone Ethan had remarked over. "Yes, that's obsidian, I can tell from here."

"Wow," proclaimed Jesse, the last one down. His voice echoed through the cavern. "Look at those drawings!"

I followed the grooves along the cave walls as the team clustered just behind me. Long sprays of wavy lines, some ending in curlicues, blew outward from a central point near the floor.

"Looks like air," ventured Ibby. "Or wind, rather."

"Look at the tiny dude." Jesse pointed at a small humanoid figure.

So low on the wall that the feet nearly rested on the cave floor, was an androgynous figure with flying hair. It had its arms bent and held aloft. A cluster of various sized circles seemed to rotate above its head and the lines of wind started not far from the figure and sprayed out, up, and away in all directions.

"I have seen wind lines made like this before on other rocks." Ethan removed his hat and wiped his brow. "I believed at the time that it represented the Ghibli."

"What's the Ghibli?" asked Ibby.

"A hot, dust-carrying North African wind. It originates here in the highlands of Libya and blows toward the Mediterranean every spring and summer. It's one of the reasons we planned our dig for spring, before the winds kick up."

The wind I had inhaled, seemingly without end, had been warm. Had the Ghibli been what I had breathed in?

Ethan continued, "I understand it is most despised by the locals. Covers everything with sand and fills the air, killing all visibility. It limits travel for months and I'm sure it seems like it will never end, to them." Ethan bent down on one knee to take a closer look at the small figure. "The Ghibli has been known to bury whole cities in one night. It's no wonder the locals fear it."

The feeling of the wind sweeping through the tunnel and filling my lungs to stretch them to the point of bursting came back and hit me like a locomotive. My mouth felt dry and my jaw seemed locked. The Ghibli had to have something to do with what had happened to me in this cave.

"Looks like they think it originates from a human," Jesse added, nodding down at the small shape carved into the wall near the floor. He'd taken a small notepad and short scrap of pencil from a pocket and began to sketch a copy of the cave art.

"Not necessarily," replied Ethan, kneeling for a closer look. "Make sure you get a close-up of that ring of discs, or stars, or whatever they are, please."

"The drawing could just be the embodiment of a spirit or something," added Ibby, tracing the head of the figure with a fingertip. "Look at the way the hair flies out from the head. Looks a bit mad."

She was right, it did seem as though the figure was demented in some way. I peered at it, noting that the feet of the figure were just off the floor and its body seemed to have a slight arch in the spine. Is this what I had looked like while I was hovering off the cave floor and receiving the strange vision? I stared at the small figure. Was it supposed to be someone like me?

Ibby, Jesse, and Ethan were all crouched in front of the wall while I stood back observing the image as a whole. My hands felt cool and I stuffed them into my hoody pockets.

"What happened here?" Ibby moved back to the broken glass.

She didn't ask it as though she expected anyone to know the answer. As far as they knew, the glass had been there for a century. I could keep quiet, and no one would know what happened to it. Already a film of dust coated the line of glass chips.

"I broke it accidentally," I said, unable to even lie by omission. "It used to be a whole piece of desert glass, embedded in the rock just there." I pointed to the empty depression. "It was the same size as the obsidian."

"You broke it?" Ethan sounded horrified, his face seemed a pale moon in the shadows of the cave. For an archaeologist, leaving so much as a crack in a bone was an offense too great to be borne.

"I didn't mean to, I—" I took a breath. I couldn't explain how I'd broken the glass without explaining that I'd first been lifted off the floor and changed. So I told them. In as simple terms as possible, and haltingly, painfully aware that I sounded crazy, I explained to them what I had experienced. "I had a sort of vision," I added toward the end of my story. All three of them had been taking in every detail of my story with incredulity. They were amazed, but even so, they handled it a lot better than I had expected. They believed me and that was comforting.

"What kind of vision?" Ethan prompted me to continue.

"I saw a man in an oasis. Maybe it was the Sahara before the desertification process began. He was a man with light gray, almost silver, eyes. It seemed like he could only move in slow motion."

"Who was he?" Ibby's voice was soft, comforting. "Who was the man?"

"Light gray eyes," murmured Jesse. "Like yours."

"I had never seen him before," I said. "But—" I swallowed, feeling raw, vulnerable. My eyes flashed to Jesse's and I nodded. "I thought he was maybe my father. There were some similarities in our faces and our hands."

Ibby put a hand out and squeezed my shoulder, picking up on my discomfort. "What else happened in this vision?"

"He just mouthed one word." My heart began to pound as the memory came back to me. The strange warning, the urgent directive, which so far I had not heeded because I didn't understand it. "Run."

It hit me suddenly that it was exactly what the security team and our diggers from Ghat had done—they had run fast and far. But they had been running from me. So why was I being given the same advice? And how could I run from myself?

Ibby's, Jesse's, and Ethan's faces all widened with surprise and their eyes darted to each other and back to me. I thought they looked rather comical, like a set of puppets.

"Run," Ethan echoed, his voice a rasp. "Run where? Run from what?"

I shrugged. "I have no idea." I gestured to the drawing on the cave walls. "The Ghibli? You said it comes in the spring and summer, right? It's almost spring now. In fact, the winds have already picked up."

Ibby was nodding, but Jesse looked doubtful.

"I've never heard the like," murmured Ethan, scratching his chin through his beard. "Run." His shoulders shook as he gave a disbelieving laugh. "Don't that beat all."

It seemed to me as though there was something artificial in his words, but I couldn't put my finger on why. Maybe it was his choice of words. I'd never heard him say an old-fashioned phrase like 'don't that beat all,' before. It struck me as weird, like a line he'd been given to speak in a play.

The light in the cave seemed to dim as a cloud either moved across the setting sun, or maybe we simply hadn't noticed how much time had slipped away while we were discussing this find.

"I'll need to call our sponsor," said Ethan, looking around at everything except for me. It seemed to me that he was now deliberately avoiding my gaze. *You're being paranoid, Petra,* I thought. He just doesn't know what to think. The whole thing is freaky and supernatural. I'd be spooked too if I were hearing my story for the first time— in fact, I *was* spooked. Overall, he was taking it very much in stride, considering.

"Let's get back to camp." Ethan held out a hand to Ibby to go up the ladder first. "We have some decisions to make."

But by the time we got back to camp, we were all emotionally and physically exhausted from the hike and the events of the last several hours. We drank more water and snacked on bread and jam sandwiches.

Ibby's jaw cracked as a huge yawn overtook her. "I don't want to miss anything, but I'm shattered." She looked at Ethan with watery eyes. "What if we talked more about what to do next over breakfast, when we're all fresh?"

Ethan nodded in agreement. Dark circles had blossomed under his eyes. "Sleep sounds wise. I couldn't do a simple math problem right now with the way I'm feeling."

Jesse gave me a small smile and squeezed my arm as we all said goodnight to one another.

I crawled into my tent and collapsed into my sleeping bag without changing into my pajamas.

FOURTEEN

I was so comatose that I would have slept through a freight train. So, when strong hands grabbed me harshly and suddenly in the middle of the night, I thought at first I was having a very convincing nightmare. I tried to scream but it stoppered in my throat where it felt like some wraith had a chokehold on my windpipe. I'd had dreams where I was unable to scream before, but this one felt *so* real. My heart exploded in my chest and a sound of choking and suffocation filled my ears. *My* choking. *My* suffocation. My eyes searched desperately for something to purchase on in the blackness. The lack of oxygen in my body jolted me fully awake and I realized with a heart-stopping fear, that I was being taken from my tent in the dead of night. I began to thrash wildly, putting all the energy I had into freeing myself to breathe. My wrists and ankles were held in a vise-like grip and all my thrashing only served to exhaust my muscles and make every fiber scream and burn for oxygen.

There was the sound of a lighter being snapped on and the flash of a small flame. Black eyes shone from an intense face. Dark, angry eyes. The eyes were desperate and fearful. The owner of the eyes was almost completely silent, and only the sound of breath being sucked in through his nose made me realize he was on the edge of panic. A soft, suffocating fabric replaced the hand over my mouth and a hand cupped my skull and pressed my face into the towel, which reeked like ammonia.

All went sweetly black.

THE WEIGHT of my body lying parallel to the earth and swaying up and down dragged me slowly to consciousness. The feeling of a bar against my wrist and my fingers trailing through air began to nudge away the fog in my brain. My head throbbed and felt like it was the size of a watermelon, full of heavy gel and pounding like a giant heart. I worked to open my eyes but they felt stuck, seamed together and fastened with glue. My mouth hurt, its corners pulled back by something jammed between my teeth and tied tightly behind my head. A gag, and the thought of being gagged and all the connotations that came along with it was the catalyst for me to force my eyes open.

The world was a blur of dim colors. A headache pulsed in my temples, different from the one I got from reading people's thoughts. Terror nauseated me and I tried to scream for help around the gag in my mouth. I sucked air in through my nose so hard and fast that my sinuses burned and my eyes watered, blurring my vision. Tears leaked from my eyes and dripped back into my hairline. I squeezed my eyes shut in an effort to clear my sight.

I was on a stretcher, which explained the way my body was being jostled. My muscles felt weak and shaky, as though it was going to require all of the power I had to lift my hand off the edge of the stretcher and ease the pain of the bar pressing against my forearm.

Blurry figures moved against a hazy background and the smell of the air told me it was early morning. My eyes opened and my vision cleared a bit. I frantically looked around, desperate to orient myself. Men clustered around a campfire. Two camels curled up in the sand behind them, munching their cuds without a care in the world. Faces turned to me, over shoulders and above other heads. Eyes followed me. Tanned faces with dark brooding eyes. Two of the faces looked familiar.

A wall of canvas cut off the faces and I fell into shade. It took all the effort I had to roll my head from one side to the other, and the muscles in my neck screamed with agony. How long had I been unconscious? Where was I? The apathy that I had woken into began to clear away as a humid morning mist burns away under the heat of a fat sun.

I sucked in a breath as fear knotted my intestines. My eyes rolled as my thoughts cleared–I had been taken from my bed. Drugged. Abducted. Fury began to build in me. Indignation that my rights had been snatched away.

Just as my eyes were gaining purchase on the two men who had carried me into this tent, the stretcher was lowered and then upturned.

With a shocked squeal through the gag, I rolled off the stretcher and landed hard on my chest and stomach in the sand. The breath was knocked out of me and I began to struggle to breathe again. My desperate gasps for air filled the tent. My arms were yanked behind my back as my body was jerked backward and upright. Sharp pains in my wrists made me gasp and finally, oxygen filled my lungs again.

Voices spoke in Tamahaq, fast and fearful. I could recognize that it was Tamahaq because I had heard our security team and our laborers from Ghat speak it.

Fear clouded my thoughts and my heart raced and burned in my chest, even my left arm was burning. Stress. I clenched my eyes shut, wondering if I might actually have a heart attack. It was that difference that I had noted in the cave that calmed me, the steady, powerful pulse of energy in my chest that reminded me that I was not completely helpless. Without opening my eyes, I reached for any thoughts near me that were not my own–probing and seeking. Who were my captors, and what did they want?

Opening my eyes, I glared up into the face that hovered just over mine. He startled at my snapping gaze and said something with urgency to whoever was behind me. They fastened my wrists together to the tent pole behind me.

I tried to say 'What do you want?' but the words were only a muffled croak against the gag.

The men began to speak rapidly, and were clearly in a hurry to get away from me. I lifted the barrier of my mind to see if I could glean anything from their minds. Their thoughts flew about the tent like bats, difficult to catch and fueled by terror. Why were they so afraid of me? I had no intention of hurting anyone. I gave up speaking and tried to catch one of these flying mental clues, but caught only words in a foreign tongue, meaningless.

In a final argument and with a spray of sand over my lap, the men left the tent as though it was on fire. They left me panting through my nose, confused, and angry. They closed the flap and blocked out most of the sun, leaving me in only a line of dim light.

I brought the barrier back down, wincing at the new headache which was building on top of the old one. My thoughts, which had been shattered and blown apart by the drug they'd forced on me, began to roll slowly back together like beads of mercury.

Three of the faces I had seen at the fire came back to me. Members of our security team. Their names pelted me in the head like someone throwing snowballs. *Mifta. Abu. Hassan.*

The memory of the people scrambling for the Jeeps and yelling *Euroklydon!* in the same tones you'd yell *bomb!* came tumbling back. These people were terrified of me. So terrified that they weren't content to just run far away and leave me be, they had to return and apprehend me in the dark of night, like thieves. They had to have me in their control. What for? Whatever it was for, it wasn't going to be good. Did they think I was the Ghibli personified? Responsible for burying their cities and suffocating the desert people over the centuries? It seemed too bizarre to be true.

I closed my eyes and leaned my head back against the tent pole.

My body ached but my head hurt most of all. I was so thirsty. My mouth felt pasty, my tongue swollen. The fabric between my teeth was stealing any moisture from my mouth. I bit down on the gag hard and in anger. The sound of my teeth grinding against the fabric was loud in my ears.

My thinking was clearing but still felt slow and sluggish. Here I was, powerful enough to lift many tons of stone with just the energy living inside me, yet I was tied up like a goat to a stake. I looked around. The tent was barren–a simple canvas sheet draped over two posts, its edges pinned down into the sand. There was nothing in here with me save the sound of my own breathing and whatever insects were living in the sand beneath me.

My mind scrambled to lay purchase on a plan of some kind. I had abilities, but they were abilities and powers I didn't fully understand. I had shattered the glass in the cave accidentally by matching its frequency with my heart. Could I do something similar here? But shatter what?

The sound of angry talk outside made me cock my head. A woman's voice could be heard amidst the men's chatter—soft and appealing, only to be interrupted and cut down. Were they talking about me?

I tried to twist my palm so that I could lay it against the tent pole, but the best I could do was press the side of my first knuckle and the pad between my thumb and forefinger against the wood. I closed my eyes and tuned in to the pole. Its frequency was dull and slow but detectable. I took a deep breath and slowed the drum in my chest to match it. The wood began to buzz and vibrate, sending out a strange din, but it didn't shatter. Of course it didn't. Glass shattered because it was brittle and inflexible. Wood didn't have this same quality. I opened my eyes and let the oscillation in my chest return to normal. The wood went still and quiet. I wouldn't be able to shatter the rope, either.

I looked down at the sand between my bent knees and gave it a mental shove. A long gouge blew through the sand, blowing particulate toward the tent door with a dry spatter. An idea took hold. I looked up at where the tent pole lifted the canvas up in a point. Focusing on the tent pole, I took purchase on it with my mind and directed the pole upward, out of the earth. Nothing happened. I frowned, confused. I could lift a huge block of rock but I couldn't lift a tentpole out of the ground? This wasn't making sense.

I repeated the experiment with the sand, this time hitting it in another direction. The sand responded and I left another gouge in the dirt floor. A pile of sand blew against the canvas wall, punching it out. I froze. That punch would have easily been detectable from the outside and I didn't want to draw any additional attention to myself. I listened, my heart pounding, but the voices had moved away from my tent and were just a murmur in the distance—and calmer now.

I looked up at the tent pole again. So why did the pole not respond to my mental command, but the sand did? I tried again, wrapping my mental fingers around the wood and applying a command for the pole to move up and out of the earth. The result was the same. Nothing. I snuffed a frustrated breath out of my nose but in the same moment, I realized that I had a solution anyway. If the tent pole wouldn't budge, but the sand would, then I could simply dig my way into the sand at its base until it toppled and I could free my hands.

And then what? Crawl out of the tent and run away across the sand? In which direction? For how long? This was the Sahara. It was the largest desert in the world. Aside from the men and at least one woman clustered around a firepit, and the camels, I took in no more information about my surroundings. I didn't know if I was near a city, like Ghat, or if they'd taken me farther into the Acacus, or across the dunes to some remote camp.

I had power, but what was I prepared to do with it to secure my freedom? I couldn't understand their thoughts or anticipate their actions, at least not unless I could find one of them who thought in pictures, but even that wouldn't provide much of a defense. I might only be able to anticipate their actions seconds before it happened, which was not enough of an advantage. And the whole time I'd have to fight the headache that came with mind-reading.

I should at least wait until dark.

What if they have plans for you before dark?

Then I'll blow sand in their eyes, try and commandeer a vehicle of some kind, and run, in any direction.

Not much of a plan, Petra.

It's all I've got.

I closed my eyes and tilted my head back against the tent pole again, to wait.

FIFTEEN

The sound of night insects roused me and I opened my eyes to the dark inside the tent. I grimaced as I moved my head, my neck muscles protesting having been bent in an unnatural position for so long. My hair tickled my face and lips and I shook my head to move it away, immediately regretting it as my neck spasmed. I wished I hadn't fallen asleep. Now I had no idea what time it might be. I listened and heard no movement, only the sound of the wind and of fine particles of sand occasionally hitting the side of the tent.

As I was struggling to my feet, the sound of the tent zipper being slid open nearly sent me into a fit of panic. I gasped and lurched back against the tent pole, bruising my shoulder blade and knocking the back of my head against the wood.

A slender-fingered and pale hand thrust itself into my vision, followed by a familiar ghostly face.

"Molly," I gasped as she freed the cloth from my mouth. I flexed my jaw and touched my dry, cracked lips with my tongue. The sides of my mouth felt like they had cracked at the seams. I took a breath to still the aching thrum of the battery in my chest.

"I'm sorry it took me so long," she whispered. "I saw them bring

you in, but I couldn't get away earlier. We have to move. Quickly."
She pulled something from her pocket. A dull gleam of metal from
the moonlight spilling in through the tent door told me it was a utility
knife, the kind you'd use to cut open boxes. She freed the blade from
where it was hidden in the handle.

I swallowed hard and went stiff as she moved behind me and cut
the binds at my wrists. After several moments of sawing, my wrists
came free. I stifled a groan of both relief and pain as agony bolted
through my shoulders and arms. I rubbed my shoulders and upper
arms, moved and rotated them to increase circulation. I crossed my
arms in front of my chest and hugged myself to stretch my cramped
upper back muscles.

Molly tucked the blade away into a pocket and clasped me by the
shoulders. Looking me in the eye, moonlight illuminating only half of
her face, she mouthed unnecessary words: "Be very, very quiet."

I nodded. My mouth felt dry as sawdust and just when she'd
given me the directive to be silent, there was a dry tickle in my throat
and I fought the urge to cough. The blood pressure in my head
increased and I covered my mouth to keep the cough in. Fine time to
have a hacking attack.

She splayed her hands on her chest, and then down to her hips, as
though looking for something. A hand disappeared into a back pocket
and she retrieved a small bottle. She unscrewed the top and handed it
to me. "Drink."

I snatched at the bottle, my throat convulsing against my will to
keep silent. I swallowed greedily and the dryness in my throat
washed away in a flood of cool water. I finished the whole bottle and
wished for more. I gave her a look bursting with gratitude. Gesturing
for me to follow her, she poked her head out of the tent and looked
about. She stepped out into the sand and reached back a hand, which
I took. I allowed her to pull me along, and our feet padded nearly
silently on the sand of the Sahara.

Under a half-moon, I was able to see my prison for the first time.
Haphazard clusters of tents and shacks crouched under the starlit sky

like hulking trolls sleeping under blankets. Jeeps and other vehicles were parked seemingly at random. The firepit I had been carried past earlier loomed like a black hole in the sand. Dark blobs of rocks for chairs formed a circle around it like it was the site of some ancient megalithic construction. Beyond, in the far distance, a yellow glow lit the sky and a thin line of twinkly lights crouched low over the desert horizon, disappearing behind dunes.

Following my rescuer, my heart in my mouth and my throat crying out for more water, I slunk from shadow to shadow until we reached a Jeep on the outer edge of the encampment.

"Get in," she whispered. "Door is open."

I couldn't have been happier to oblige. I hooked my fingers into the seam behind the door and pulled it open silently. Slipping my butt onto the seat, I realized then that my whole body was shaking with fear and adrenalin.

Molly was already in the driver's seat. She looked over at me in the dark with a broad grin of white teeth. "Don't close the door yet," she said, and I nodded, holding the door open a crack with my hand, the way she was doing.

When she started the engine, I held my breath, half expecting an angry mob to materialize out of the sand and chase after us, waving machetes and rifles in the air. Thankfully, that didn't happen. We closed our doors as she rolled the Jeep in a half-circle, the lights off, and then straightened the wheels until we were heading down a sand dune. The camp was swallowed up in darkness behind us.

She flicked on the lights and illuminated the desert ahead. Tire tracks led away into the distance over rolling dunes, as far as the lights could show us.

I swallowed and then coughed. "Do you have any more water? I'm parched."

She jabbed a thumb at the back seat. "Behind you."

I twisted to look in the back seat and saw a cluster of bottles. I grabbed one and had the cap off and was gulping greedily before I'd even turned around.

"Poor thing." Molly made a clucking sound, then barked a disbelieving laugh of relief. She shook her head. "I've seen some things in my day." She didn't have to add that she'd never seen anything quite like my kidnapping.

"I have so many questions." I said between gulps. My mouth was sore but already starting to feel better thanks to the water. "Thank you for rescuing me."

"I couldn't just leave you there." She shot me a look of sympathy.

"Well, thank you just the same."

She grunted. "We had some boys come in from your security detail. I wouldn't have known who they were if I hadn't joined your dune-skiing party that day." She frowned and shook her head again. "They were all freaked out and talking fast. I couldn't understand a thing they were saying. Next thing I know, you're being carried through camp with a gag on. Just when you think you know them," she tsked. She grasped the wheel tightly as we rolled over some short, steep dunes. "I'll take you back to Ethan, but my suggestion is that you get back to civilization as quickly as possible."

My stomach dropped at her words. She sounded like she knew something. "What were they going to do with me?"

She blew out a long breath. "I can't say for sure, but it wasn't good. There was an argument. Some of them think you're an incarnation," she waved her fingers, "the desert wind personified, or some such nonsense. My Tamahaq isn't very good. It's a tough language. There was a name for this wind."

"The Ghibli?"

"That's the one. They call you Euroklydon." She scanned my face before looking at the horizon again. The tires hit the bottom of a dune and we began to climb. "Half of them say you should be destroyed. Others are terrified and want to let you go before you destroy the whole camp. They didn't want to anger you." She barked the same incredulous laugh she had given off earlier. "They think you're some kind of vindictive goddess!"

"And the rest?"

"The rest keep quiet. Either they don't believe it or they don't know what to think." She made a sour face. "I won't be invited to finish my research after this stunt, but I'm so glad I was there to put a stop to this craziness."

"Me too. You never ran across this myth before?"

"I think I have, it was just outside the scope of my research so I didn't pay due attention. Sure, I wish I had in retrospect. What I can tell you is that the sub-groups that make up the Tuaregs don't always see eye to eye. It's a volatile relationship at times, but one thing they mostly agree on is that this Euroklydon deity exists and it's a thing to be feared." She reached back and grabbed a bottle of water, untwisted the cap and took a long drink. She set it in the cupholder by her knee. "If I were studying the mythology of the region I could tell you more. But you're the archaeologist, right?" She shot me a discerning glance. "Albeit a baby one. You know anything about this," she waved her fingers as though doing a magic spell, "Euroklydon?"

I shook my head. "No, not really. We found a cave drawing of a figure that could be it maybe, but even Ethan says Euroklydon occurs only a few times in ancient texts. It refers to a tempest." I shrugged and watched the sand dunes roll under our tires. We crested the long dune and began to descend the other side.

I wasn't about to confirm that I had any abilities at all to Molly. Until last week, Euroklydon was a myth I would have enjoyed reading about in my pajamas with a cup of tea, just one more local legend to enrich my understanding of the history and culture of the area. Now? I passed a hand over my face and closed my eyes. My mind was whirling so fast it was giving me vertigo. Could I actually be Euroklydon?

"Tired?"

I nodded.

"Have a sleep." Molly patted my knee. "Your seat goes back. I'll wake you when we reach your camp."

I lay my seat back and did just that.

"WAKE UP, PETRA." The soft words were accompanied by a light jiggle of my shoulder. My necked creaked painfully as I opened my eyes and lifted my head to look out the windshield. The headlights of the Jeep illuminated the tracks in the sand before us. Darkness swallowed the world around us save for a sprinkling of stars overhead. I was about to ask where we were when a familiar finger of stone loomed in the beam of the headlights. We were nearly back to camp.

"Your team is probably beside themselves with worry. If Ethan hasn't already mobilized a search party, I'm sure he's on it," Molly said. She picked up my water bottle and held it out in front of me. "Drink. You're still dehydrated."

I took the bottle and swigged the rest of it back. I looked over at Molly in the dim blue glow of the Jeep's electronics. She had already said she wouldn't be able to finish her research.

"What are you going to do?" I asked. "Where are you going to go?"

She shrugged. "I'll go to Ghat and call Boston. We'll sort something out. Don't you worry about me. I'll find some way of finishing my research, even if it's not where I started it."

"I'm sorry your project has been derailed." I could imagine just how gutted I would be if I had to abandon an excavation. Then I realized that was precisely what I might have to do.

"It's not your fault," she said, slowing the Jeep to a crawl as we passed through a narrow section of the canyon. "I'm glad I was there to help. I have all my notes with me," she jerked a thumb toward the back seat, "so there's that at least." Her eyes widened as she saw the long stone monolith lying across an excavation trench in the headlights. "That stone was upright the last time I was here!"

"It fell."

Molly gave me a surprised look. "No one was hurt, I hope?"

I shook my head, but I was distracted by my own thoughts. "No. Do you think they were planning to kill me?" I blurted, twisting the cap on and off my water bottle.

She slowed the Jeep further and glanced at me. "I don't know," she answered softly, "but from what they were saying, it didn't sound good. One of them suggested that killing you might put a stop to the seasonal winds that have taken so much from them year after year."

I frowned. "If they hate it so much, they should consider moving out of the Ghibli's path."

"It's not that simple."

I looked out the window into blackness, seeing more of my own warped reflection than the world on the other side of the glass. "I know," I murmured. It was difficult to feel empathy for the people who could so cold-bloodedly execute a teenage girl using such an archaic and superstitious rationalization. Then an ironic smile tugged at the corners of my mouth.

Molly spied my expression from my reflection in the window. "What's funny?"

I faced her. "I want to study archaeology because I'm fascinated by ancient cultures and ways of life. They were our ancestors and progenitors. Their societies laid the groundwork for ours. I have always had respect for the ways that spiritual beliefs and divinity impacted how they lived and behaved."

Molly returned my smile, already making the connection before I pointed it out. "But now that it's personal, it's suddenly more difficult to esteem."

"Yeah."

"I know what you mean. I wrote my thesis on the Aztecs. It was easy enough to read about the blood sacrifices with clemency. But if I suddenly found myself at the top of a pyramid with a knife over my heart?" She shuddered and didn't finish.

The headlights fell on the tents of the camp and two shapes standing in front of the fire pit turned to face us. Ethan and Jesse. A third shape emerged from the shadows of a tent and Ibby crossed the sand toward them, watching us approach with a hand lifted to shield her eyes from the headlights.

Molly pulled the Jeep to a stop and turned the vehicle off. When we got out and the muted glow of firelight hit our faces, a cry went up. The look on Jesse's and Ethan's face was of pure relief and I was thrust through with a powerful feeling of gratitude for the obvious care they had for my well-being.

I had grown up with a sort of suspicion around people's affections. Was my therapist just concerned about my well-being because he wanted to give an improved report to the government about how I was doing, or did he really care? These were the concerns of a young child and pre-teen, paranoid musings that came about as a result of unusual circumstances and caregivers who were not family. It was very clear from their expressions that my dig-team genuinely cared about me, and the feeling both startled and warmed me all over.

"Petra! Molly!"

"Oh, thank God!"

Chris and Sarah joined us around the fire and I was surrounded by my dig-mates and swallowed up with hugs and firm pats, as though they wanted to verify that I was in fact real.

Ethan wrapped Molly up in a bear hug. "We owe you so much. We didn't even know where to start." He gazed at Molly and I realized he was actually misty-eyed. "Thank you for what you did."

"Anyone would have done it." Molly's cheeks were visibly pink even in the firelight.

Ibby handed Molly a bowl of soup and held a second one out to me. "Eat, both of you. Then talk."

I hadn't even realized how hungry I was, but the moment the minestrone touched my tongue I was unstoppable and consumed my soup in moments. I didn't even normally like minestrone.

"Slow down, Petra," said Jesse from where he sat near my knee. "No one is going to take it away from you."

I gave him a chipmunk-cheeked smile.

"What happened?" demanded Ethan. "We've been going out of our minds."

Molly explained that members of a nearby camp, the camp she'd been conducting her research from for the past several months, had taken it upon themselves to nab me in the night and tie me up in a tent until they could decide what to do with me. Some men had appeared in camp the day before talking about Euroklydon. "I recognized Mifta and Hassan, but I didn't know what they were so upset about."

"Our security team." Ethan shook his head at the irony of the situation. "I didn't realize superstition still had such a stronghold here."

Molly's brows shot up and she let out a belly laugh. "I can assure you, superstition is as hale and hearty as it has ever been. You study the leavings of the dead, but I study the living. In many ways, nothing has changed for thousands of years. Just because we have satellite phones and quantum computers doesn't mean antiquated beliefs are a thing of the past."

"Fair enough. But what were they planning to do with her? Kill her?" Jesse scoffed.

Molly and I looked at one another, and Jesse saw the understanding that passed between us.

His face widened with horror. "No," he said, looking from me to Molly and back again. "No way. They wouldn't!"

"This is the part where I tell you to get her out of here," said Molly, her face serious. "They will know how she escaped in the morning, if they haven't discovered it already. They will not be happy about it. I can't speak for what they might do."

"Where will you go?"

"I have friends in Ghat. Besides, it's not me they're after."

"They wouldn't attack us," said Ethan, alarmed. "We have permission to be here. We've been sanctioned."

"Do you think they care about that?" Molly stood and put her hands on her hips. "What they believe is that the seasonal winds that have been responsible for destroying their properties year in and year out"—she held her palm out toward me as though presenting me on a stage to a crowd—"has finally taken her fleshly form. You will not be able to reason them out of believing this. Most of them have been convinced that an end to her is an end to their enemy. Send her home. Immediately."

I swallowed. "I can't go home until we're done. I need credit for this excavation." I looked up at Ethan. "Can we bring in more security?" I regretted the words as soon as they left my mouth. It sounded like I was willing to risk the safety of everyone on my dig-team just for a line on my resume that would look good. "I'm sorry," I added. "I take it back."

"I can ensure that you get full credit," said Ethan quickly.

I shook my head, pushing my hair back from my forehead with frustration. "That's as good as lying," I said. "I won't take credit for something I didn't see through to its conclusion. If what Molly says is true, then you should send me home."

Jesse put a hand on my shoulder and squeezed. He knew what this dig meant to me, he would have been in this position not so many years before, trying to earn a spot at the University of Australia.

I stared miserably into the fire. Questions burned inside me. Why did this have to happen? *Was* I this Euroklydon the people feared?

"That settles it, then," said Ethan. "I'll arrange for a flight out of here for Petra."

"I would recommend you all go," said Molly. "Come back in the fall when all this has blown over, sorry, no pun intended. It'll just be safer that way."

"What about our sponsor?" Jesse moved to stand behind me, hands on my shoulders. The heat of his palms was comforting. "Will we be able to get the funding next year?"

Ethan shrugged. "I would have to discuss that with Jody. They might take these extenuating circumstances into account. The most important thing is that we don't take any unnecessary risks." He nodded to Molly. "Thanks for your recommendation. We'll take your advice."

"Good." Molly nodded. "Then I'll be on my way."

"You must be exhausted. You're welcome to stay here for the

night," Ethan offered. "We'll erect a tent for you. We have enough bedding for thirty people here."

But Molly shook her head. "I'm wide awake. I'll be fine." She looked down at me. "I wish you good luck. I don't know why the Tuaregs are so impressed by you, but," she shrugged, "there is plenty I have yet to understand here."

I got up and gave her a hug. "I owe you." I walked her to her vehicle. "Do you happen to have a card or something? I'd like to touch base with you once I get home."

Molly opened the Jeep door and retrieved a pen and a small notepad from the glove compartment. She wrote down her information, tore off the page and handed it to me. Then she got in, closed the door, and rolled the window down.

"Don't linger." Molly looked up at me with a pleading look. "I have been here for nearly a year and I have never seen them fear anything the way they fear you. These people are proud, but something about you is making them do things I would never have thought they'd do. Take it seriously." She put a hand out of the open window and squeezed my arm. "Be safe."

I put my hand over hers. "You too. Ethan gave you his sat phone number?"

She nodded. "I'll let him know when I've arrived in Ghat."

"Okay." I watched her back the Jeep and turn it around, the headlights making strange shadows dance across the stones. The taillights dimmed as the vehicle drove away and the Jeep finally disappeared behind the rocks.

SIXTEEN

I came awake like a cat in the dark, thinking for certain I had heard something unnatural.

Clawing my way out of my sleeping bag, I scrambled from the canvas womb and emerged outside, blinking in the light of early dawn. The dream had returned. The visual of the silver-eyed man I couldn't help but think of as my father seemed burned into my memory. It was as though I could still see his face overlaid against the morning sky, and I could still read the urgent warning on his lips.

Run.

The horizon was painted in pretty tones of peach and pink, and the sand appeared red. The air was fresh and already hazy with the promise of heat to come. The sun was low on the horizon and partially shrouded, but it was already fat and hot and would soon burn the clouds away.

Movement in my periphery drew my attention to Ibby's tent. I watched as she emerged, her dark hair a tangled mess, her face splitting with a yawn.

"What's happening?" She pushed her hair back from her face and wandered over to me. "Are you all right? I heard you yell."

I had yelled?

"I thought I heard–" I paused, listening.

Ibby tilted her head. Our gazes locked as we both listened. Her beautiful bronze eyes widened. She'd heard it too: the sound of engines, vehicles coming across the desert, drawing nearer by the moment. Fear wrapped its cloak around me and the instinctive urge to run and hide was nearly overwhelming.

"Trucks!" Ibby's bark made me jump. "Everybody up! Get up now!" She moved faster than I would have thought possible for a woman who'd been dead asleep only moments before. She bolted to the dining tent, ripping back the canvas door. I heard the sounds of rifling through cupboards, of plates and silverware being violently disturbed.

Moving on instinct and curiosity, I followed her. She seemed to have had an idea, which was more than I could say for myself. I watched her overturn a basket and yank another from its home on the shelf. She was making a mess of Chris's previously tidy kitchen.

"What are you doing?"

"What do you think?" She threw me a wild look. She yanked on another bin and picked a large knife out of it, holding it up somewhat dubiously.

"Ibby." My eyes widened. "We don't even know who it is or what they want yet. But whoever they are, they'll be more likely to be friendly if you're not waving a ten-inch butcher knife at them."

"Don't be naïve." But she dropped the knife.

Ethan, Chris, Jesse, and Sarah had all been roused from sleep and had gathered near the firepit. Ibby and I joined them, watching the headlights of two trucks approach.

"Why do I feel like I want to grab a weapon?" I heard Jesse mutter to Chris under his breath. "We don't even *have* any weapons anymore, now that our security team abandoned us."

Ibby and I shared a look. Tension crackled through the air like lightning.

"It would only inflame the situation. I'm sure whatever it is they want, they can be rationalized with," replied Chris, quietly, eyes on the trucks.

Jesse shot Chris an incredulous look. "They *kidnapped* her!"

Jesse moved to stand in front of me but I put a hand on his arm and stepped around him. I wasn't going to hide behind anyone.

"Petra," he whispered and I felt his fingers brush my shoulder. He stepped up behind me, so close I could feel his heat.

The trucks slowed as they approached and I counted the heads I could see. Five men and ... and a woman. I gasped as the vehicles came to a stop, their wheels sliding on the sand, ploughing up little dunes.

Doors opened and men got out. Molly was dragged roughly out of a vehicle. With a gag between her teeth and her hands tied behind her back, she was a sorry sight. A red mark had blossomed on her cheekbone and one eye was puffy.

"*Now* do you wish I'd grabbed a weapon?" Ibby muttered as she moved to stand beside me. Anger was rolling off her in waves. Her fingers flexed at her sides.

"What's going on here," barked Ethan, stepping forward. He was trying to be brave but his voice sounded weak and old. "Release that woman! At once!"

My heart sank at the lack of confidence in his voice. The poor man was a field director, not a soldier. He wasn't trained to handle confrontation like this. It was why we'd been given a security team. My heart ached with sympathy for him.

All five men had their dark eyes trained on me. Mifta's was the only face I recognized. All five of them had their jackets dangling open and I knew without a shadow of a doubt that they were all armed. My heart was tripping along like I'd had way too much caffeine, and my mind raced to come up with something that would defuse the situation.

"Mifta." It took effort to keep my voice clear and strong. I stepped in front of Ethan, sending a signal to everyone that I was not afraid— at least that's what I hoped was coming across. I kept my eyes on

Mifta's alone. He had seen me move that instrument with my mind, I felt sure of it now. Maybe he had been waiting for this moment ever since then, planning some way to capture me. Now that his first plan had failed, he was past being stealthy. The gall of he and the men with him astounded me.

Mifta's eyes held mine but his face was turned slightly away from me, like he was afraid I was going to explode. "We won't hurt her if you come with us. We want only you."

Jesse barged forward. "You can't just *take* people." His voice was rough and hard. "You can't have either of them. Molly hasn't done anything wrong. All she's done is saved a woman you stole in the middle of the night." He spat at Mifta's feet. "Like a bunch of cowards."

"Jesse." I reached out a hand to stop him but he blocked me, coming between Mifta and me with his bulk. Jesse's hands clenched into fists. His movements were inflammatory, and full of fury. Everyone stiffened and the tension ratcheted further.

The man holding Molly pushed her down in the sand. She went to her knees with a muffled cry and bowed her head. His hand snaked into his jacket from which he removed a gun.

"You stop," he barked at Jesse. His voice was low, liquid and heavily accented. "I shoot her!" He followed this with a stream of Tamahaq and pointed the weapon at the ground near Molly's knee. His arm was straight and tense and ready to shift and make the iron weapon bark, changing the moment forever.

Jesse went still, glowering at the man with the gun.

The wind lifted the sand and swirled it around us, making everyone blink. For an endless moment we were a frozen montage of bodies, forever stuck in a stand-off. Forever waiting to see who would make the first move.

It had to be me. I was the one they wanted. They had no interest in anyone on my team, only me. But I had no intention of ever being under their control again.

The pulse of my heart slowed and became a hum. The fear

that I had woken with burnt away like dry autumn grass as the waves pulsed through me. My fingers throbbed with heat and energy.

"What did I ever do to you?"

Mifta answered. "For thousands of years you have destroyed our cities, our homes—"

"She's not the Ghibli," sneered Jesse. "She's just a girl."

The corner of Mifta's lip curled ever so slightly. "She is not just a girl. You know this. You saw her—"

"We saw her save our lives," Ibby interjected. "She is special, no one is denying that. But she's a nineteen-year-old kid from Canada. She's never even been to Libya before. It's crazy to think that she—"

"She is Euroklydon." Mifta spat the name.

The vibration inside me began to speed up, originating at my heart and building in my body like a charge. I had no desire to hurt these men. They were misdirected, mistaken, that was all, but I wouldn't let them hurt Molly or anyone else. I most certainly wasn't going to give myself to them. If I had been given this power for any reason at all, it was to prevent something bad from happening in this moment. But a question simmered under all the racing thoughts and loosely forming plans—why hadn't they shot me by now? We were all unarmed, they could see that.

"Her, for you." Mifta's brow had begun to shine with sweat. "Decide." He leveled his gun at Molly's head. She squeezed her eyes shut, her lips pinched between her teeth. The man on her other side stepped back and lowered his weapon, letting Mifta take control of Molly.

"What happens once you've shot her, Mifta?" Ethan spoke up.

"It'll be on your head," Mifta answered, still looking only at me. His face was solemn and resolute, but as we glared at each other, his face began to twitch with effort.

Mifta glanced down at the gun, which was twisting in his hand, slowly. His eyes flashed accusingly to me and back down again and he uttered some harsh words in Tamahaq. The barrel was now pointing up, above Molly's head, continuing to twist backwards, slowly pointing to the sky.

"What's happening?" Jesse stepped up beside me, his voice quiet. "What are you doing?"

"I'm not doing anything," I hissed. I checked myself, but nothing had changed, no power was leaking out of me, though the thrumming inside me had only increased.

One of the other men yelled in Tamahaq and his voice was joined by the others, all shouting at Mifta. Fear was deforming their faces. Mifta yelled back, his tone defensive, and it seemed there was an argument going on.

Molly, still on the ground, looked up, her eyes wide as she watched the gun twist unnaturally in Mifta's trembling hands. His eyes bulged with effort to get control of his weapon.

One of Mifta's companions nailed me with a look of terror, and understanding. He thought I was doing this. His hand reached into his coat.

"Nope," said Jesse and he darted forward as another gun appeared in the man's hand. He made to raise it toward me, but before he could aim properly, Jesse was on him. Jesse grabbed the man's wrists and shoved the gun skyward.

CRACK!

The gun fired into the sky as they wrestled, and suddenly everyone was moving. The gun's retort had broken the spell.

I dashed forward to Molly as Mifta began to yell commands, his face pouring sweat. He had no choice but to release the gun which was forcing his hand back into a painful and unnatural angle. As he released it, the gun hovered in the air by itself.

Molly, Mifta, and I all stared at it, shocked. Mifta's eyes flashed to my face, accusatory, but when he saw that I was just as surprised as he was, his fear turned to terror.

The gun flew sideways and landed in the sand several feet away, as though someone had swatted it with a baseball bat.

BANG!

The sound of another gunshot made the three of us jump like we'd been electrocuted.

Jesse sent a fist into his opponent's face and the sound of bone against skull set my teeth on edge.

Mifta dove for the gun lying in the sand and without thinking, I gave him a hard mental shove. Heat radiated through me. Mifta went flying forward, past the gun and headlong into the sand.

Suddenly, everyone was running and it was utter chaos. I grabbed the gun and covered Molly as she ran toward the cover of the mountains, hands still bound. She disappeared behind the van and I hoped she kept running farther into the mountains. There were countless crevices and caves to hide in beyond the campsite.

I spun, looking for Jesse, and found him just as he was hit across the jaw with a fist. He went sprawling, twisting to catch himself and landing awkwardly with an arm pinned under his chest. Anger bolted through me as I watched the militant turn the gun on Jesse as he lay in the sand, his mouth bleeding.

Flicking my hand, I sent a rushing twist of energy into the sand at the man's feet. He staggered backward and raised an arm as a wall of sand flew up in his face, swirling around him, peppering his skin and clothing. Jesse scrambled up and out of the way. He ran straight for me, grabbed my wrist, and shoved me ahead of him toward the network of crevices.

The sound of shouting made me look over my shoulder for the other three men, who were nowhere to be found. It sounded like orders were being belted, like Mifta was trying to get his men organized. I thought I heard the sounds of static punching off and on.

"Are you okay?" I tugged on Jesse's shoulder as we entered a narrow canyon, out of sight of the campsite.

Jesse nodded and turned back, examining my face. "Are you?"

"Yes. Just—" I sucked in a breath and put a hand on my driving heart.

"In shock?" He put an arm around me and squeezed. "Come on. Keep moving."

I nodded. "Where is everyone?" I followed him deeper into the mountains.

"Hiding from the fools with guns," Jesse panted. "What do you think?"

Running footsteps behind us made us both gasp and turn, hands coming up defensively. I half raised the gun, although I doubted I could have ever fired the thing. Jesse's fists clenched, ready to fight. But it was only Ibby who appeared.

"Whoa!" She held up her palms. "Easy." She spied the gun in my hand. "Nice work."

We wound our way through the narrow canyon as it led us on a semi-circular path around the perimeter of the campsite. Stopping to rest and listen, we stared at each other, panting and wide-eyed.

"This is crazy," Ibby whispered, wiping the sweat from her brow with her pajama sleeve. She hadn't even had a chance to dress properly before we'd been set upon. At least she'd pulled on a pair of sneakers. "What happens now? We have no weapons. I think that guy was calling for back up on a radio!"

"I thought I heard static." I frowned. We were already outmatched. We couldn't handle more one-minded, misdirected militants. Things were plenty ugly enough.

"We need to get out of here before more of them arrive," whispered Jesse. "They're totally irrational."

"But how?" Ibby crossed her arms over her chest, like she'd become aware of how poorly dressed she was for the situation.

"Listen," I hushed them, and they fell silent.

The sound of additional vehicles approaching made Ibby's jaw drop. She gaped at us. "How did they get here so fast?"

"They must have been waiting." Jesse wiped the sweat from his forehead and touched a finger to his swollen lip, wincing. He pressed his sleeve against his lip, leaving a small bloodstain. "They were planning it this way the whole time."

"What are they going to do now?" Ibby whispered.

The sound of gunfire made all of us jump, but it wasn't the single bark of a pistol, but the repeated rat-a-tat of an automatic weapon. Ibby and I clamped our hands over our ears. The gun went silent, leaving us sweat-beaded and pale.

My mind raced. Had they just executed someone? Or had they fired into the air to scare us?

We listened, barely breathing, to the sound of voices conversing in Tamahaq. Truck doors slammed, there were the sounds of men in action, men with urgent purpose. I had to do something. I was the only one of our team in possession of anything that resembled a form of defense.

A tap on my shoulder brought Jesse to my attention. He beckoned to Ibby and me to follow him deeper into the rocks. Not that long ago, Jesse and I had run on top of these stones under a sky spread with stars. Not that long ago, I had fallen into a hidden cave and been made different. That night seemed like years ago.

Following Jesse as he snaked his way through the rocks, we skirted the campsite. The sounds of men at work grew louder. He stopped us at a place where the boulders made a lumpy natural ladder.

"We can get a look from here," Jesse whispered, and began to climb.

"Wait." I grasped the back of his shirt. "I'll go."

He peered over his shoulder and shook his head vigorously, a slash between his brows.

I nodded my head more vigorously, and pulled him down.

Ibby and Jesse shared a look. I didn't miss the nearly imperceptible nod that passed from Ibby to Jesse, as though she was telling him that it was indeed smarter to have me go. I had mysterious powers, Jesse didn't.

Jesse frowned and let me pass. "Go slow."

I nodded and began to climb.

Once I'd crawled high enough, I pressed my belly against the rock and squirmed forward until the campsite came into partial view. What I saw made my pulse jump. I counted six more vehicles—and those were just the ones that I could see. But it wasn't the vehicles themselves that made my breath catch; two of them had their back seats ripped out and large guns mounted on the back. No one was manning them, but the fact that they were there was plenty enough reason for my heart to rattle wildly against my ribcage.

Men swarmed the site, most of them carrying weapons and strange-looking devices. A few metal trunks lay open on the sand and a man in fatigues knelt in front of one of them, talking with three others. They pointed and made gestures with their hands as they talked, likely discussing the geography of our site and how it factored into whatever they were doing. More men approached and weapons were distributed from the trunk. At least, I assumed they were weapons. I didn't know what else they could be.

I squinted, trying to get a better idea of what they were carrying. Whatever the objects were, they were partially encased in a cylindrical white casing. A metal bar protruded from the center. I cautiously lifted the gate on my mind and probed the thoughts of the man kneeling in front of the metal trunk. Instantly, the base of my skull began to throb. Like a spatter of hard-driving rain into my forehead, I received a stream of words that made no sense.

I slammed the gate down again, squeezing my eyes shut against the pain. I laid my forehead down on the back of my hand and took a few breaths. The pain eased slowly, the way sunlight leaked out of the sky after sunset.

The man whose thoughts I had tried to read was communicating, not visualizing. I should have known better. I lifted my head, searching for someone else I could read. Zeroing in on a man jogging across the campsite with two of the devices in his hands, I lifted the mental gate again, hoping for visuals this time.

I started as I saw myself in his mind. In his imaginings, my body hung in the air, and my hair was aflame. A burning black and red mushroom cloud billowed upward behind me. An explosive backdrop outlined my form, seeming to lift and carry me. Strangely, my legs were pumping as though I was running on the hot drafts of air from a detonation. I did not look as though I was hurt by the explosion, but rather exalted by it. This confused me more than anything else. Why would he imagine me this way? Powerful? Alive?

My head throbbed and I dropped the gate between us again, taken aback. I put a hand to my forehead and then rubbed the back of my neck as the pain eased.

If his imaginings were telling, the devices had to be explosives. Were they planning to blow us all up?

My body pulsed against the rock beneath me and I lay my head to the side, taking deep breaths. Surely not. Surely they were not planning to set bombs off just to flush me out? They'd kill everyone here, and destroy our entire excavation, just for me?

Maybe I'd misunderstood the situation. This couldn't really be happening. It made no sense.

Another question popped up—did they know about the cave where I had touched the stones? It was the only other thing I could think that they might be trying to destroy. If that was their intent, they were way off base.

Movement off to my right caught my eye. A man carrying three of the explosives passed behind one of our trenches and disappeared into a crack in the rock. I watched for him to come back out, assuming he'd gone in to deposit the bombs. My hand flew to my mouth as Chris came out of the rock with the man following behind him. The man carried no explosives, but he wielded a weapon.

Chris had his hands on his head, fingers interlaced. He stumbled through the campsite, face pale. The man who'd rousted him from his hiding place passed Chris into the custody of a fellow militant and disappeared back into the rocks. Poor Chris was bound and made to sit cross-legged against the tire of a truck. He was pale and his eyes darted around the campsite, likely on the hunt for anyone who could help him.

One of the men knelt in front of Chris and asked him questions. Chris merely shook his head. The man questioning him raised his voice and grabbed Chris by the hair, pushing his head back against the truck, hard. At the sound of the back of Chris's head hitting the metal body of the truck, something in me broke. This could not go on. An oscillating hum filled my mind as power began to build inside me.

I pulled myself the rest of the way up the rock and got to my feet.

"Petra!" Jesse's whisper was loud and fierce. "What are you doing?"

I ignored him. I no longer cared if I was seen. Let them see me. I had something to show them. I would be still no longer.

The wind began to pick up because I willed it to. I looked at Chris sitting on the ground, his mouth downturned, his expression twisted with fear. He didn't deserve this. None of us did. The wind increased. The canvas of the tents flapped and popped. Granules of sand swirled through the air.

Someone shouted in alarm. One of our opponents, who had been carrying a metal box across the campsite, looked up and spied me. He now stood frozen on the sand, squinting up at where I stood looking down at the scene below.

One by one, the men stopped moving, and all of them looked up. Chris let his head rest against the side of the vehicle and I saw his lips mouth my name. Oddly, all the fear left his features, like someone had rubbed an eraser across the lines between his brows. His mouth even twitched with the suggestion of a smile and his eyes locked onto me, hopeful.

I clenched my teeth at the scene below me. Men were all over the place were equipped and intent on destruction, they'd parked their vehicles haphazardly and their footprints had raked up the sand of our dig site. The string perimeters of our trenches, so carefully put there by Ethan, were torn away. The guns in the backs of the truck were ready and waiting to send out sprays of deadly bullets. And for what? Because of a superstition? Some misdirected hypothesis that the teenager now standing on the stone above them was an incarnation of an ancient and punitive god? Where did this leave me? Forced to defend myself and my friends and colleagues, forced to confirm that I had the powers they so feared. What choice had they given me but to become what they were so afraid of?

They expected a vengeful wind, and a vengeful wind was what I would give them.

There was a pop of gunfire. A bullet whizzed by my head. I spied the gun and the man behind it, lying on his stomach in the sand. He took aim a second time. I flicked a hand with a snap and a bellowing twister of sand sprang up and swallowed the man from view. I relaxed and the grains fell, making him visible once again. He was nothing but a head poking out of a man-sized molehill of grit, clenching his eyes shut and spitting.

KA-BOOOM!

I dropped to my stomach as something exploded behind me. The sound was huge and thick, almost guttural. My eardrums sucked inward as the air changed. A sudden blast of hot air slapped over me, strong enough to have knocked me flat if I hadn't already been on my belly.

Glancing back while keeping my cheek against the rock, I could see black smoke billowing up from a crevice in the mountains. Flaming pieces of rock arched through the air and fell among the terrain and the campsite. The canvas of the tents snapped like bull-whips. The air tasted metallic and smelled like smoke. Blood and fury beat in my head.

I caught the frightened faces of Jesse and Ibby as they peeked up from the crack. I held a palm out at them, *don't move.*

That blast, had it been closer, could have killed someone. For all I knew, it *had* killed someone. I didn't know where Ethan, Molly, or Sarah were hiding. It had been only a single explosion but I had lost track of the bombs ferried out of the metal box and distributed.

I hopped to my feet and with a hoarse, angry cry, I chose a vehicle and shot my palm forward like I was batting away a projectile. There was a sharp creak and the sound of metal denting. One of the Jeeps with a gun in the back lifted high into the air. It turned end over end three times as it flew away from the campsite and landed upside down with a crash in a dune beyond the tire tracks. Its tires spun uselessly and reminded me of the way a beetle stuck on its back thrashes its legs.

My wind picked up sand and whipped it into the air. Cries from the men became faint as the gale howled like a living entity. I could sense the air; I could feel where it was and how much power it had. It wound and spun through the rocks and through the excavation site like a living thing. It was as though it knew my enemies, for the wind did not disturb the dig pits, or behind me where Ibby and Jesse were hiding. It made a pocket of protection around Chris even as it pummeled the others it found, throwing them through the air as they reached for weapons or ran for cover, their hands protecting their heads and faces.

I slapped away the vehicle behind Chris. In his own bubble of stillness, not a hair on his head was disturbed. He turned and watched the truck arc into the air. Before it landed, I hit it again, volleying it high and spinning into the air. Random objects flew from its open windows. It smashed against a cliff face, glass shattering. Chris watched this, frozen, then peered back at me. I couldn't be sure but it looked like he was grinning.

I punched at three more vehicles in succession. One fell straight back and tilted up on its bumper before flipping over backwards. With a scream of twisting metal, another tumbled end over end like a weed blowing in the wind until it landed on its side, looking for all the world like a giant hand had crunched it like an aluminum can.

I spied a man army-crawling across the sand from behind Chris's van toward a crack in the mountain. With a sweep of my hand, I buried him with enough sand to keep him busy for a while.

Our van jostled and squeaked as sand filled the air. Two tents came unpegged and the canvas spiraled into the air like kites. Someone's pillow was caught in a cyclone and whirled in a circle up high over the desert and out of sight.

Ghostly shapes appeared in the sandstorm, lifting up from the ground and from cracks and crevasses around the campsite. I blinked in confusion at these until I realized they were guns and bombs and other metal objects such as dig tools, thermoses and cookware. They hovered, unaffected by the sandstorm, but being lifted by some unknown force all the same.

A sound turned my head.

"Ibby!" I cried out as she stepped up beside me. "Get down!"

She shook her head. Her eyes were locked on the site below us. With a wave of her arms, all of the metal objects—bombs, guns, and dig tools—moved together into a cluster. They began to make a pile on the sand in the middle of our campsite, unaffected by my whirling storm. The clank and ting of metal against metal was muffled by the sound of wind and blowing sand.

I watched, my jaw going slack. I closed my mouth with a snap and looked at Ibby, who was now relaxed and staring back at me. I realized then who had twisted the gun out of Mifta's hand.

I was not the only supernatural being here.

"You can stop the storm now." Her words bounced around our little bubble of safety. "They can't hurt us anymore."

I looked down at the wreckage. Vehicles were shattered beyond repair, lying in heaps across the desert and at the base of basalt cliffs. A pile of weapons and bombs lay on the sand. Sand shifted where men worked to dig themselves out before they suffocated. The sky was yellow and opaque with clouds of swirling grit. Wind screamed through the cracks and valleys of the mountains, whistling and furious.

I relaxed, and the winds died immediately. The sound of sand raining down and spattering filled our ears. Slowly, the sky shifted from a brown haze to a clear blue. The campsite fell into silence.

Jesse climbed up and joined us, eyes like saucers. The three of us stood and surveyed the damage for what seemed like a very long time.

SEVENTEEN

The sound of tires on sand made me lift my hands again, heart jumping, eyes on the desert horizon. But the trucks that raced up to the dig site and slammed on the brakes, spitting sand from their tires, their noses dipping as they came to a halt, were not like the other vehicles. These were two white Escalades, decked out and glimmering with chrome. The logo on the sides had the letters 'TNC' emblazed on the white paint.

"It's Miss Marks," said Ibby. "Thank God."

I blinked at her. "Jody Marks? Our sponsor?"

She nodded, and her hands relaxed to her sides. "Ethan would have contacted her when you went missing." Ibby tilted her head back to the sun and closed her eyes. Sweat shone from her brow and beaded across her upper lip.

I stared at her, still processing the fact that she'd been keeping her secret from everyone all along.

"Why didn't you tell me?" I asked, quietly.

She opened one eye and squinted at me. "Same reason *you* kept yours a secret, too."

One corner of my mouth tugged up. "Touché."

"Come on." Jesse made his way off the rock and turned to help Ibby and me climb down. The three of us snaked through the crevasse back to the campsite.

Chris was on his feet and came running across the sand to hug me. Sarah, Ethan, and Molly emerged from their hiding places. I was relieved to see everyone was okay and someone had cut Molly out of her bonds.

A tall woman in dark glasses and a white scarf wrapped over her head and across her mouth got out of the passenger's side of the Escalade. A slim Asian man with exquisite cheekbones got out of the driver's side. He too wore dark glasses, but I could see his eyebrows arch above the frames of his glasses as he looked around the site.

A third Escalade, this one with a light blue paint-job, pulled up and parked beside the white ones. Two more people joined the tall woman. One of them was broad and dark, with skin the color of coffee. The other was a petite redheaded woman in glasses and a white pant-suit. They were speaking to one another in low voices.

The tall woman in the white scarf walked toward us and stopped in front of Ibby and me. "Everyone all right?"

She took off her glasses and studied us with teak colored eyes. Her skin was smooth and unlined, but the bangs poking out from under her scarf were light gray. The nearly white strands caught the sun and turned to silver.

There was a murmur of sounds which made it seem that yes, everyone was alive, but everyone was also so dazed at the day's events that they didn't know what to say. Everyone took their turns gaping at the pile of metal on the sand and the wreckage of vehicles scattered across the desert.

"Hello, Ibukun," the woman said.

"Miss Marks," Ibby replied, her voice respectful.

I looked from one to the other, surprised that they knew one another. Ibby had never said anything about knowing our sponsor personally.

"How many were there?"

"Hard to say for sure," said Ibby. "At first there were only five, but after they called for backup," she shrugged, "maybe a dozen more. Right, Petra?"

I nodded. I felt Jesse join me and slip an arm around my waist. I smiled up at him and he gave me a squeeze.

"You okay?" he asked.

I nodded. "You?"

He nodded, but his face was pale and serious.

Miss Marks yelled at her team and they spread through the camp, weapons drawn. They began to flush out our attackers, all of whom were dusty and sandy from head to toe. The attackers were led to kneel in one place where the largest of Jody's team stood over them. The strangest thing was that they all seemed relaxed at this point, almost as though they were relieved the battle was over. A few of them sent me furtive glances, but their fear was not as palpable as it had been before. It was like a spell had been broken now that someone had taken charge.

"How did you get here so fast?" I asked Miss Marks. "And with a whole team."

Miss Marks put a hand around my shoulders and Jesse fell back. "Ethan radioed me when you went missing. I had flown into Alawenat to meet with the team leader scheduled to come in for the fall. I left Alawenat thinking we had a kidnapping of a supernatural to deal with." She let go of me and gestured around us at the mess. "Clearly that is no longer the case."

I gave her a puzzled look. "How did you know I'm a supernatural?"

"I radioed her after you lifted that rock and saved your team-mates." Ethan came walking up to us, his face shining with sweat. Dark circles stained the armpits of his shirt. "If it weren't for you, I have a feeling this whole site would be burning rubble by now." He looked around. "It's a mess, but the pits are nearly unscathed. Remarkable."

Miss Marks crossed her arms and looked at me. "You are very

lucky that TNC happens to be sponsoring this dig, instead of some other corporation or authority."

"Why's that?" I asked, really not sure what to think of this woman.

"Because. Supernaturals are part of our business," she said simply. "We already have the infrastructure and processes in place to protect your identities and provide you with a whole safety network and the technology and opportunities to hone your abilities. For instance. Ibukun is an Inconquo, a metal elemental," she said pointedly, jerking her chin toward Ibby. "She works for us."

I stared at Ibby in shock and she gave me a small smile and an even smaller nod.

"An Inconquo?"

Ibby nodded again.

"I have so many questions—"

"And you," Miss Marks interrupted, putting the stem of her sunglasses between her teeth while she pondered me. "Your kind is new to us. But Ethan tells me the locals here refer to you as Euroklydon. Had you ever heard that term before?"

I shook my head. How was it that this woman knew everything about the situation already? There was no awe or any kind of surprise on her face at what had been revealed to everyone out here in this remote desert location.

"They are quite afraid of you," she said with a smirk. "Probably wise. Come on." She opened an arm out toward the Escalades. "Let's get you home. We have much to discuss, and I suspect the locals will be happy to see you gone."

"What happens now?" I asked.

"We get you out of here, as quickly as possible." She tilted her chin down and looked at us seriously from under her silver brows. "And then we have a talk about your future."

Ibby and I looked at each other. Ibby gave my shoulder a reassuring squeeze. "It's all a good thing. Trust me."

"What about this mess?" I gestured to the disaster the dig site was in.

"The team will clean it up and more help is on its way," Miss Marks said. "We have more important things to concern you with than sweeping up sand and wrecked vehicles. If you agree to what is on offer, your life will change for the better, I can promise you that."

When Ibby began to follow Miss Marks toward the Escalades, I followed too. I looked back over my shoulder to see Jesse watching me with a frown on his face. I smiled at him and it seemed he tried to smile back but failed.

I wanted to run across the sand toward him and throw my arms around him. I wanted to talk through everything that had just happened. I wanted to kiss that serious look off his face. But he made no move to follow me or to come and say goodbye. He saw we were being whisked away and seemed rooted to the sand.

Jesse only watched as I got into the blue Escalade behind Ibby. I felt numb and distracted by the sudden turn of events. In that moment, I thought that Jesse proved to be just as I had always warned myself he was. Uninvolved. A flirt. A fair-weather crush. All that talk of traveling to Petra together, or visiting Australia to see where he was from, was exactly what I'd suspected it was. Talk.

Still. It stung.

IBBY and I were whisked away to Alawenat, examined by a medical team and pronounced well, and then put up in a hotel room until our respective flights. Everything happened so fast that I barely had time to think. I hadn't even been given a moment to say goodbye to Jesse, Ethan, Chris, Molly, or Sarah.

My personal items were waiting for me in my hotel room when I returned from my physical. By the time I had been fed a wholesome meal and had a rest, I fully regretted not making the move to say goodbye to Jesse. Maybe he was just a spring crush, but we had shared something significant, and I thought that at least I deserved a goodbye. Why did Miss Marks have to rush us out of there so fast?

Why hadn't she even thought to suggest Ibby and I would like to say goodbye to our dig-mates? The more I thought about it, the stranger it seemed.

I rooted out the contacts sheet everyone had been given on the day of our briefing, and dialed Jesse's number. There was no answer, but I wasn't overly surprised at this. The number was an Australian cell and he probably hadn't even arrived back on Australian soil yet. For all I knew, he was on a plane.

Someone knocked at my hotel door, so I folded away the page with all the phone numbers on it and got up to answer it. Ibby stood before me.

"Hey," I said. "How are you? Everything okay?"

She nodded and came in when I gestured her forward. I sat down on the bed, and she sat down across from me.

"Do you know where Jesse is?" I asked. "Or any of our team, for that matter?"

"Miss Marks told me they've been sent home and given some pay to allow them to recover from what happened."

"We didn't even get to say goodbye to them," I grumbled.

"No. It certainly hasn't been business as usual around here. I guess you've got a flight home booked for tomorrow morning already."

"Really?"

She nodded. "TNC doesn't waste any time, and Jody Marks in particular."

"What about you?"

"My plane leaves tomorrow afternoon."

"Back to London?"

She nodded. She bit her lip, looking at me like she wanted to say something important. "I have wanted to explain things to you."

I pulled my legs up underneath me, crossing them. "Okay."

"I've been working for Miss Marks for a year now. I'm not an archaeologist. I was brought on as a sort of undercover security agent. There is supposedly some artifact of huge significance buried somewhere at that site. Having five security agents is already unusual for an excavation. Miss Marks wanted to bolster security even more without making it obvious."

I blinked as this sank in. "Because you're"—what had Miss Marks called her?—"an Inconquo?"

Ibby nodded. "She didn't want anyone to know, so I wasn't allowed to say."

"But why?"

"Well, I'm a supernatural, so my identity is supposed to be kept secret. I'm only telling you this now because you're a supernatural, too. And Miss Marks is probably going to offer you a job."

"I sort of gathered that from what she said at the site. What kind of job?"

"I have no idea," Ibby said. "But whatever it is, you should take it. TNC pays extremely well and you wouldn't believe the technology they have. There are whole rosters of supernaturals who work for them."

I let out a long breath. "But my dream is to be an archaeologist."

"They won't stand in the way of that, Petra," Ibby said. "If anything, they'll try and facilitate it for you."

"Do you know why they didn't let us say goodbye to everyone?"

"You can call them. I see you've already tried," she said, looking at the folded page of telephone numbers beside my phone. "Jesse?"

I nodded miserably. "No luck."

"He's probably on a plane. Try again tomorrow morning."

I fell back on the bed. "Everything has just been happening so fast. My mind is spinning."

I felt Ibby's hand squeeze my knee. "I know. That's why they'll let you go home and rest for a while before they call you in."

"Call me where?"

She fell back down next to me and looked over, quirking a smile. "TNC has field stations all over the place. Wherever it is, it'll be state-of-the-art. Even if you decline their offer, you should go just to see it."

I nodded. "Miss Marks seems nice."

"She's a professional," said Ibby. "And she'll treat you like one, too."

"But I'm no professional. I'm just a confused teenager."

Ibby shook her head. "You're a supernatural. There's a whole world of supernaturals out there. It's time to take your place among them."

EIGHTEEN

Less than a week later, I got the invitation Ibby was talking about.

"We'd like to bring you to one of our facilities to have your abilities tested," Miss Marks's voice came through the phone. "Would you agree to that? We can help you make sense of your nature."

"I would appreciate that," I said, tapping a pencil nervously against the blank page under my hand.

"There's a helicopter pad behind the fire station. We have clearance to pick you up there. Do you know where the fire station is?"

"Yes." I'd never had reason to go there before, but...my brain was running a million miles a minute. I'd expected a bus ticket or maybe a cab. But she was talking about helicopter pads.

"A pilot will pick you up tomorrow at seven a.m."

Inside, I was flabbergasted. A freaking helicopter would pick me up? This was unbelievable. Trying to recover, I asked, "Should I bring anything?"

"Just you. We'll deliver you back home before nightfall. And Petra?"

"Yeah?"

"Try to book off work the next day. You'll be tired."

WE PASSED over miles and miles of forested wilderness, the shadow of our small insectile helicopter skating over the tops of the trees like those little bugs that can float on water. Just as it seemed as though the woods would never end, I spotted something small and dark with sharp edges nestled in the forest. The sunlight reflected off tall square windows and flashed in my eyes, making me blink.

A modern looking building with a blacktop helicopter pad came into focus. The building looked as though it had been constructed out of dark gray modular blocks of sheet-metal. Whenever they'd needed more space, they'd simply tacked on another room, the way schools added portables to their parking lots.

Off in the distance I caught a glimpse of a large patch of deforested earth. I squinted to get a better view, thinking I could see earth-movers and the tiny forms of men moving about the bare ground. But as the helicopter landed, the patch disappeared behind the trees and out of view.

The helicopter landed gently on the pad and powered off. The whirring blades began to slow. A figure appeared in my window. A man in a suit jacket and jeans approached the helicopter. The small door to my right swung open and he held a hand toward me to help me down. We smiled at each other. I thanked the pilot, and he saluted me with a deadpan expression. I got out and followed the man to a set of steps leading down to a terrace.

"I'm Andrew Banks," said the man, holding a glass door open for me. "You can call me Banks. Everyone else does. How was your flight, Miss Kara?"

"Amazing," I replied, passing into an air-conditioned hallway lined with plain gray doors. "I'd never been on a helicopter before. You guys travel in style."

"Yes, we know how to do it right." Banks nodded politely to a woman in a dress suit as she passed us.

"So, you'll take me to Miss Marks?"

"Not today," replied Banks. "You'll meet with Hiroki Emoto today. He's one of our scientists."

"Oh. He'll do the testing?" That made sense, that a scientist would do it rather than a businesswoman. "This is a satellite office, right? Where are your headquarters?"

"Like most big tech firms, we're headquartered in Silicon Valley but we've got satellite offices all over the world."

Professionally dressed people (why they bothered to dress up when this whole set-up was in the middle of the wilderness was beyond me) walked this way and that, each of them on a mission. A few of them were in fatigues and looked as though they did the majority of their work out of doors and with their hands. They stood, heads bent and talking with their nicely dressed colleagues. No one noticed me in my jeans and plaid button-up shirt, trailing along behind Banks.

"Miss Kara, this is Hiroki Emoto," said Banks.

I stopped abruptly and with a flush of embarrassment. I'd been gawking everywhere and not watching where we were going.

A slim man with blue-black hair and a set of striking and familiar cheekbones said, "Hello, Miss Kara. Welcome to Field Station Eleven."

"You were in Libya!" I blurted, happy to see a face I recognized.

He gave me a close-mouthed smile. "Yes, I was." He held a hand out. "Wonderful to see you under better circumstances. Call me Hiroki."

I shook his hand. "You too. And call me Petra."

"You know each other. Good. I'll leave the two of you then," added Banks, and strode away.

"This way to the lab, Petra," said Hiroki, leading me through another set of double doors and down a long glass hallway that linked two modular buildings. We were suspended over the tops of trees and I gaped down through the glass under my feet, watching the tips of the pine trees pass by.

"Can I ask you something?"

"Of course," said Hiroki as we made our way through the halls.

"Is there some reason I haven't been able to contact one of my friends from the dig?"

Hiroki frowned. "Not that I know of, why?"

"No reason. Just haven't been able to reach someone I really wanted to say goodbye to." I didn't say more to Hiroki, but I was still quite upset. Over the last week, I had called Jesse once a day, with no answer. I only had the service of a simple landline, I had never splurged on extras like voicemail. If he had called while I was away, I wouldn't have known it. I tried not to think that he was just going to vanish from my life, the way everyone else I'd ever cared about had done, but the thought was like a ghost in the corner of every room.

"You have an amazing office," I said, clearing my throat and pushing thoughts of Jesse out of my mind.

"Thank you," Hiroki replied. "We like it. No distractions. And our new chef is a master of filet mignon," he added over his shoulder. "Not like the last guy." He gave an exaggerated shudder.

The elevated glass hallway ended and we took stairs down to ground level where a set of metallic double doors barred the way.

Hiroki took off his glasses and peered into a glass square shining a dim blue light. A bell went off and a panel near his belly button lit up. He pressed a thumb to the lit pad and a loud click told us we could go inside.

"Welcome to my lab," Hiroki said with no small amount of pride. "This is my playground."

I grinned at him as I stepped through the doors, eager to see what I was capable of. Noel hadn't been able to help me, what seemed ages ago when I'd walked into his office, but these people knew supernaturals. With a feeling of homecoming, I stepped into the lab.

NINETEEN

I stood in the middle of a busy street. I was the only still thing, my feet in my white sneakers on wet pavement. It wasn't raining anymore, but the air felt thick and humid and clung to my skin, and it curled my hair. Faceless people, busy and paying no attention to the frozen girl, brushed by me. They carried groceries, brought cigarettes to their lips, laughed and talked as they rushed by. Children barely visible in the edges of my periphery carried balloons which bobbed along; the bright colors looked like big cartoon heads. The crowd moved so fast that my hair moved with their passing, their shoulders jostling mine.

Out of a faceless, heedless crowd, a man materialized. The same silver-gray eyes. My jawline. My brow. His every movement came as though he was walking through molasses, agonizingly slow. Even his expression changed only subtly, languidly. We locked eyes like we were crossing swords.

I know who you are, his eyes said. His face was relaxed.

And I know you.

His face began to change, slowly, from impassive to insistent. His brows drew together and down, his mouth opened and lips tightened.

My heart surged, as though our emotions were linked. I felt a panicked urgency, but didn't understand where the fear was coming from. My brow felt warm, my cheeks flushed. The crowd jostled me. Their bodies began to hit mine harder, striking me and pushing me back. I began to lose sight of the man I had come to think of as my father as the crowd came between us. His face appeared one more time, over someone's shoulder. He seemed as one stuck in another dimension, where the seconds moved so much slower. The word finally formed on his lips and I did not want to read it.

Run.

I reached a hand out toward him and was horrified to discover that I couldn't move normally either. My arm lifted with intention to part the crowd, so I could find him again. My own fingers appeared in my periphery, then my hand appeared. But it appeared not as a flesh and blood hand. I looked down, my horror deepening. My entire hand and arm were made of sand, and the sand was breaking apart and blowing away, making little eddies of dust in the air.

I jerked awake and sat bolt upright in bed. Spring rain sprayed against the windows like there was a firehose pointed at the side of my apartment building. My heart hammered and I put a hand to my chest. My mouth was as dry as the Sahara. I threw the covers back and went to my tiny bathroom, barely registering how cold the floor was. I turned on the water and dumped my toothbrush out of its cup. I filled the cup and drank deeply—one, two, three cups of water.

I looked into the mirror, almost afraid of what I would see there. Would I be made of sand? My worried eyes met the eyes of the girl in the mirror. She looked normal, made of flesh, only distressed and a bit damp around the edges. I brushed the moisture off my brow.

"Why?" I asked the girl in the mirror. "Why did I see him again? Why run? Run from what?"

I had defeated the militants in Libya and now I was home, oceans away. What did I still have to be scared of? Why did this vision still plague me?

Exhausted, I went back to my bed and crawled between the

sheets, telling myself that Hiroki would have some answers for me soon. I had told him about the dream, and he had listened quietly and patiently. He didn't seem surprised by it. He assured me that one day the meaning would come clear. I only hoped that it became clear before it was too late.

I tried to imagine what life might have been like for me if I had been left to figure out my abilities all on my own, and the thought of it sent red-eyed rats of terror running up and down my spine. As strange as it was to be thrust into this new world of supernaturals and a corporation who employed and developed them, I was grateful that I didn't have to face it alone.

EPILOGUE

Jody looked up from the papers on her desk as a knock sounded on her office door. Hiroki was visible through the glass window, looking pale. She waved him in. He stepped into the office and approached Jody's desk.

"So, what did you find? Was the testing of our asset a success?" Jody gestured that Hiroki should sit in the plush chair across from her. "Take a seat. How are you feeling? You look ill. You know there's been that bug going around."

Hiroki sat and took out a handkerchief to wipe his brow. "I wish you'd call her Petra, or Miss Kara at the very least."

Jody folded her hands on the desk in front of her. "We know where that can lead. Two years you've been working for us and you're still not accustomed to the language. We have it for a reason, you know."

Hiroki nodded. After a moment's thought, he rose and went to the water cooler in the corner. The nearby window overlooked miles of treetops, no civilization for a very long way. His hand shook as he took a cup and filled it.

"Are you all right?" Jody's voice was filled with real concern now, as though it had finally clicked that Hiroki was either very stressed or sick. "Did something happen?"

Hiroki gave a sarcastic laugh before chugging a full cup of water and filling a second.

"Hiroki, you're scaring me."

He arched a brow. "I thought nothing scared you."

"Figure of speech. Will you quit stalling, please? Does Devin need to be here for this?" Jody laid a hand on the mouse near her computer.

"You'll call *him* Devin, the billionaire owner of this cutting-edge tech company, but you won't call Petra by her name."

"Hiroki—" There was finally a warning in Jody's voice.

The scientist took his cup and returned to the chair to sit. He nailed Jody with a look and Jody's arms prickled at the fear she saw there.

"You're terrified," Jody said, quietly. Her tone was filled with wonder and respect. "She is everything we thought she would be?"

"She's more." Hiroki slammed the second cup of water back and crushed it in his fist. "I barely even know *how* to test her. She is way beyond anything I have ever seen. She's not like any of the other supernaturals we're tracking or have on staff." He threw the broken cup into the trash can and put fingertips to his temple. "She defies categorization."

"No, she doesn't." Jody sat back and tented her fingers. "They are all definable. They always come with their own sets of rules. She'll be no different. As long as we understand those rules, we'll know how best to deploy her."

Hiroki dropped his eyes. "You don't know. You weren't there."

"So, tell me what you discovered." She shot him a warning look. "And don't give me any of that scientific gobbledygook. We all know you're smart. Layman's terms please."

"Well, we started with a simple EMF measurement—"

Jody held up her hand. "I don't need to know what you did, I need to know what you *learned*."

Hiroki chewed his lip, thinking about how best to explain. "I don't even know where to start."

Jody sighed. "How about with air? The Libyans called her Euroklydon. We already know she can manipulate winds. So why don't we start there?"

Hiroki nodded and rubbed his eyes vigorously and then held his hands out, tense. "Okay, yes. She can manipulate air, but here's the strange thing. That rock that she levitated in Libya..."

Jody nodded and leaned forward, eyes glittering. Now they were getting somewhere.

"You might think that she did that with the air, because after all air pressure, if there is enough of it, can lift a heavy load. But in order to do that she would have had to condense a huge amount of air into a very small space and then shoot it at the stone in a way that lifted and held it steady. She would have to take that air from somewhere, and everyone in the vicinity would have felt and heard that. But no one noticed a thing."

"So? How did she do it if it wasn't with air?"

"Sound."

Jody's face registered surprise, then understanding. "Sonic levitation?"

Hiroki nodded. "Even mainstream archaeology is becoming more open to the theory that the pyramids and other historic structures made with megaliths could have been built using acoustic levitation."

"But no one heard anything when she levitated that rock."

"Because the frequency she would have used to do it is outside the range of human hearing. Plus," his eyes narrowed, "scientifically, I don't know how this is possible, but I think she's able to dampen the sound of the frequencies she produces. Perhaps a self-preservation technique she's not even aware she has."

"Okay, so she can lift really really heavy things—"

"That's just the start of it." Hiroki paled again as he remembered the way the needle on the Geiger counter swung abruptly over to the right side of its face and quivered there as if it wished it could go further. "Our planet has a measurable frequency. It was discovered by Schumann and recorded at 7.83Hz. We also have the ability to record the frequency of waves transmitted by the human brain. The frequency of the planet and the frequency of alpha waves from the brain is the same — 7.83 has been shown to be the pulse of life itself. With me so far?"

"Think so."

"Petra is somehow able to detect and discharge any frequency she wants to." Hiroki sat back.

"So?"

"So?! She's like a supercharged cell phone tower with a powerful magnet inside it. Even that description falls far short of doing her any justice. If she wanted to, she could wipe out millions of humans with the right transmission." He leaned forward to emphasise. "Into the *air*." Hiroki wiped an agitated hand across his mouth where sweat beaded on his upper lip. "She has freaking *chryptochromes* in her body!"

"What are those?"

"They're the protein found behind the eyes of birds. It's responsible for sending their brain a visual of the earth's magnetic field. They see something like what a fighter pilot sees to help them fly. I don't think Petra actually sees it in her vision, but she is subconsciously aware of it."

"How do you know she has chryptochromes? You'd have to dissect her to know that for sure. Wouldn't you?"

"They may not be exactly like the ones birds have, but there is no way she could do what she does without some kind of protein in her body that provides magnetic information to her brain."

"So," Jody began to count off on her fingers. "She's telekinetic—"

"Not technically," said Hiroki, holding up a palm. "She is in the sense that she can move things with her mind, but she's not actually moving the *thing*, she's using either the air around that thing, or sound to do it. It's got nothing to do with picking up or moving a solid object and everything to do with manipulating the environment around it."

"Okay." Jody continued counting. "She's aerokinetic. She's able to sonically levitate large, heavy bodies. She can discharge or read any frequency she wants. She can 'see'"—she made little quotation marks in the air with her long fingers—"the earth's magnetic field. Which means, what?"

"She's a catalyst for radioactivity." Hiroki's voice was low and hoarse.

"You measured her radioactivity?"

Hiroki nodded. "I didn't think she could do it, but as soon as I explained the difference between sound and radio waves..." He opened and closed his mouth like a drowning fish before pushing his glasses up the bridge of his nose. "She felt a heat spot on her right shoulder blade right before the needle jumped."

Jody cocked her head, confused. "A heat spot?"

"I know, I was confused by it at first too, until I realized that her back was *angled toward magnetic north*."

"Wow," Jody breathed, sitting back against her chair and putting her fingertips over her lips.

Hiroki sat back, finally satisfied that Jody seemed to be appreciating the immense discovery he'd made in Petra. "I haven't even told you yet that she can read minds."

"We knew that to be likely," Jody said, folding her hands together and letting out a long breath. "Please tell me you took the proper precautions?"

"I didn't fall off the back of a turnip truck yesterday, Jody," Hiroki snapped.

Jody cocked her head as if to say, *excuse me, peon?*

"Sorry," he apologized. "It's been an intense day."

"No doubt," she murmured.

"Yes, we did know that she was likely telepathic, what I'm interested in is *how* she does it. As you know, we never got the chance to test her father before—"

Jody interrupted Hiroki nervously. "You tested her? On telepathy?"

"Yes, with a volunteer from the research lab. Petra didn't want to do it. She says it makes her head hurt."

"But she did it."

"Yes. She did it. She can turn it off and on. She said that it took her a long time to learn how to do that and her childhood was a bit whacked out because of it. The funny thing is that her telepathy is linked to her ability to pick up frequency. I don't think she would have one without the other."

"How so?"

"Thoughts have mass and energy. When you form an image in your mind, the energy from that thought sends out tiny transmissions. Petra," Hiroki paused, "I mean the *asset*, can receive those transmissions and whatever it is inside her that's receiving it, translates it into images and thoughts, not unlike the way a computer translates zeros and ones. Hence," he waved a hand, "her brand of telepathy."

"We'll have to be careful with that," murmured Jody.

"You think?" Hiroki said sarcastically. "You're not actually thinking of signing her, are you? After everything I've told you?"

Jody blinked in shock. "And allow a competitor to pick her up? Are you crazy?"

"You're crazy if you hire her. She's un-coachable! We have no one on staff who can train her properly. We don't even know the full extent of her abilities."

"We'll have to deal with her as best we can," said Jody, her hands disappearing into her lap.

"Jody!" Hiroki gaped at her. "Have you not heard anything I've said? She's a weapon of mass destruction!"

Jody didn't hesitate. "Good thing she'll be on our side, then."

Hiroki's jaw sagged. "This is a bad idea," he whispered. "She's a really good person in spite of what she is."

"What are you saying? That she won't *want* to work with us? Aren't we *good*?"

Hiroki's jaw worked but he didn't respond.

Her voice sharp, Jody asked, "What would you suggest then?"

Hiroki took a breath. "I would terminate her."

Jody belted out an incredulous laugh and stared at her colleague, amazed. "You want me to call her by her name instead of *the asset* and in the same breath you're passing her a death sentence?" She looked at him and shook her head. "Maybe you understand how we operate better than you let on."

"I'm telling you. Signing her is a terrible idea, and letting her out into the world to be picked up by someone else is also a terrible idea." Hiroki hated himself for his own thoughts, but no one person should have the kind of power this girl had. The power she'd demonstrated in the desert was a walk in the park for her, if his findings were correct.

All laughter done with, Jody said, "We're not going to kill the most powerful supernatural we've ever come across, Hiroki. Every time we take one on there is risk involved, and this asset is no different. You know what we've set out to accomplish, or at least, some of it. I'm beginning to think we can't do it without her. She is just what we need. She could save us years."

"So what are you going to offer her?"

"That's not even an object." Jody shuffled through the papers on her desk, found a file folder and opened it. "She wants to go to Cambridge University and study archaeology." She tossed the folder back on her desk. "We'll pay for all of that, every expense she has, for as long as she needs it. We'll pay for her PhD. We could afford to pay for her to start her own archeological society if that's her dream."

Hiroki had seen Petra's eyes when she talked about this dream. Jody would be able to sell her a contract without even blinking. Petra *would* sign. Hiroki had no doubt about it. "You'll ask her for the requisite first-year commitment to start?"

"Of course."

"What would you even get her to do?"

"Nothing, initially. But I have spoken briefly to Devin about this and he feels that she would be the perfect choice to recruit for us. We have our eyes on a few others."

"She'd be brand new. She wouldn't even know what she's recruiting people for."

"She doesn't have to know. Not exactly. We give her just enough information to be compelling, it's our modus operandi, you know this." She shot Hiroki a superior look. "I hope you don't think you're any different. We only tell you what you need to know."

"I know," Hiroki murmured. It was one thing that could be counted on in this company. Secrets were essential to the ultimate success of the vision, and that was no secret.

Jody took a pair of specs from her desk and perched them on her nose before clicking her laptop to life. "We've been watching three other assets very closely. Well, four actually." She waved a hand dismissively. "But the fourth is not of interest to us, so she is inconsequential."

Hiroki blinked at this. "An inconsequential supernatural? I didn't know that was possible. What is she?"

Jody tilted her head back to look at the screen through her bifocals. "She's referred to as a Hanta, I believe. Some kind of...spirit elemental?" Her face was etched with disdain. "I don't even know what that is. Doesn't matter. Devin isn't interested in her."

"And the others?"

Jody brightened. "The others are remarkable. A trifecta we simply must have on board. Between the three of them, they can manipulate water, earth, and fire."

"Wow! Alphas?"

Jody nodded smugly. "Every one of them."

"How did you find three of them?"

Jody shot him a soppy grin. "They're friends. Isn't that sweet? That means if we get one, we get them all."

Hiroki paled with shock. "We've determined that the ratio of supernatural to natural runs around fifty million to one. That means at any given time there are only around one-hundred-fifty supernaturals in the entire world population, and that's probably optimistic. Four of them are *friends?*" Hiroki shot Jody a doubtful look. "That's near impossible."

"Actually, there are five if you include the fire asset's brother," Jody said, reading from the screen.

"What?" Hiroki leaned forward as though belted in the gut. "Can't be!"

"Mm-hmm," Jody said. "He is of some interest to Devin, but he's low-grade and too young."

"I thought he liked them young. For training."

"Only orphans," explained Jody. "This asset has a stable family life. And because his sister is of interest to us, we would start with her, anyway."

Hiroki sat in his chair dazed while Jody continued to scan the classified files on her screen. "Petra is perfect for this job," she murmured.

"Don't you mean *the asset*," Hiroki said weakly, absently.

"Yes, right."

"Why is she perfect for this job?"

"Two reasons. One is classified. The other, I haven't told you yet. Aside from being close to their age, the three alphas we want are all from Saltford. The asset's own hometown."

Hiroki held his hands wide. "Of course they are. Another improbability." He shook his head and covered his eyes with his hand. "I have a headache."

"Yes." Jody agreed with his mathematical assessment and ignored his bodily complaint. "We have research looking at Saltford. That little city has something strange going on. But I'm not going to look a gift horse in the mouth. Miss Kara can collect them in a butterfly net." She smiled, pleased.

Hiroki stared at Jody. She was so confident, so oblivious to the risks. Either that or she was aware of them but they just didn't bother her. Jody had referred to Petra by her name again, but he didn't point it out. "How are you going to suggest she does that?"

"When they're all together of course."

"Like, grabbing some fast-food or going to movie?"

"No, of course not," Jody said. "They'll have to be alone. We know they've all spent the summer away. Teenagers need their friends more than they need their parents. When they arrange to have the inevitable get-together to catch up, something teenagers like to do, I'm told"—Jody gave Hiroki a wolfish smile—"that will be our moment."

CONTINUE *to the exciting action-packed ensemble novel* ***The Elementals!***

AFTERWORD & ACKNOWLEDGMENTS

Thank you so much for taking this journey with me. You've made it to the end of *Born of Air* and you're still reading, awesome!

Born of Air, which was a particularly difficult story to conceptualize and write. Huge thanks goes out to Teresa Hull (my wonderful editor), Glenn Ricci for the excellent archaeological notes (I know so little about Saharan archaeology, I was sure to blunder this without his help), to Daniel Wiegert for helping to make the ER scene authentic, to Andy Palmer for the excellent feedback on Euroklydon as a paranormal creature, to Andrea Gleason for feedback on a realistic conversation with a therapist, to Nicola Aquino for her excellent work with consistencies and timing, and to Lisa Waters, Ruby Baty, and Karen Lubbers for proofreading. Thanks to my circle of supportive beta readers, friends and family!

Born of Air was tightly plotted along with the next book and leaves open some loops which will get closed in the last story of *The Elemental Origins Series* called simply *THE ELEMENTALS* and will bring all your favourite characters together for one exciting ensemble adventure! Read on after this letter for a sneak peek at the story.

Keep in mind that though the *Elemental Origins Series* (unofficially dubbed '*The Born of* Series' by readers) will be concluded, the characters have further adventures beyond this ensemble story. Targa's series '*The Siren's Curse*' and Georjie's series '*Earth Magic Rises*' are already out!

Visit www.alknorrbooks.com to sign up for my newsletter and be the first to learn about new releases as they come out.

Thank you, as always, for reading!

A.L. Knorr

Made in the USA
Monee, IL
07 November 2020

46957371R10105